THE

Simon Van ⋯⋯⋯⋯⋯⋯⋯⋯⋯⋯⋯⋯⋯ of London.
He is the autho⋯ ⋯⋯⋯⋯⋯⋯⋯⋯ ⋯ives of People
⋯ove, Father's ⋯⋯⋯⋯⋯⋯⋯⋯⋯ ⋯⋯⋯ The Illusion of
⋯⋯⋯eness. I⋯ ⋯ is the editor of three philosophy books and has writ-
⋯⋯ ⋯⋯ The New York Times, Guardian, Telegraph, Financial Times and
the BBC. His work has been translated into seventeen languages. He
lives in Brooklyn with his wife and daughter.

PRAISE FOR *TALES OF ACCIDENTAL GENIUS*

'There is a deep and abiding humanism to these stories: people assist-
ing others because the alternative is too grim to contemplate...For
all of the globe-trotting and experiments in storytelling found here,
there's also a very human core to these stories – a humanistic reminder
of the connections we all share.'   *Minneapolis Star Tribune*

'One of the beauties of all Van Booy's stories...is that he tells his stories without affectation, but ever so effectively as a stylist and a devout
humanist. One amplifies the other, making his stories literary trea-
sures.'   *Portland Press Herald*

'One of the best living short story writers gives us a collection of six
beautifully written stories and a novella that search for the genius in
common places and everyday deeds by way of poetic prose.'
          Kansas City Star

'A moving, humorous and engaging look at the ways people lean on
and support one another...[an] enthralling collection.'
          Paste Magazine

'From minimalistic sentences he wrings out maximum impact, strip-
ping away artifice and elaboration in favor of stark, emotional clarity
and honesty.'   *Boston Globe*

'One of the most fascinating and arresting literary stylists writing
fiction today.'   *Maine Press Herald*

'The uncanny beauty of Van Booy's prose, and his ability to knife
straight to the depths of a character's heart, fill a reader with wonder.'
          San Francisco Chronicle

ALSO BY SIMON VAN BOOY

FICTION

The Secret Lives of People in Love

Love Begins in Winter

Everything Beautiful Began After

The Illusion of Separateness

Father's Day

NONFICTION

Why We Fight

Why Our Decisions Don't Matter

Why We Need Love

PLAYS

Hindsight

TALES OF
ACCIDENTAL
GENIUS

SIMON
VAN BOOY

ONEWORLD

A Oneworld Book

First published in Great Britain and Australia by Oneworld Publications, 2016

Published by arrangement with HarperCollins Publishers, New York,
New York, U.S.A

ISBN 978-1-78074-971-6
ISBN 978-1-78074-972-3 (eBook)

Printed and bound in Great Britain by Clays Ltd, St Ives plc
Designed by Katy Riegel
Rolls-Royce illustrated by Michael Gellatly.
Illustration on page 182 by musri/iStock by Getty Images.

Oneworld Publications
10 Bloomsbury Street
London WC1B 3SR
England

Beloved friend Barbara Wersba

Contents

The Menace of Mile End

MR. BAXTER WAS the only private resident on a London street of men's tailors and barbershops.

His small house, once home to the St. James's Church clergy, was built in 1762 against the back wall of the church, between Piccadilly and Jermyn Street.

Whether by accident or inspired planning, the church sometimes appeared to embrace the little house, with two brick arms uniting in their ambition to form a spire.

During an emergency renovation in the 1960s, an unexploded bomb from World War II was found in a sewer beneath the church, and the Jermyn Street shops were evacuated for several hours. A few of the more senior tailors were reminded of the Blitz, when people in the shelters shared bars of chocolate or took turns on a cigarette.

Although Mr. Baxter had lived on Jermyn Street for eighteen years and did not speak to anyone regularly, he was well-known to his commercial neighbors by sight.

At first it was his sheer girth and height that caught their attention, and for a long time, they called him "The Giant of

Jermyn Street." But then one of the barbers recognized Mr. Baxter from years ago, when he was in the tabloids and known by a different nickname.

After almost two decades, those who worked regular hours on the street, from Floris to Turnbull & Asser, had grown so use to their residential neighbor that when he passed their windows every day on his walk home from St. James's Park (blocking out the sun for a few seconds), it was not his size they noticed—but a falling trouser hem or jacket in desperate need of a "sponge and press" or the flapping sole of a size 14 brogue.

Despite his age, Mr. Baxter was still heavily muscled, with enormous hands kept awkwardly at his sides. His eyes were a deep blue and quicker than his body, making him appear more nervous than he actually was. There were no longer any traces of brown in his hair, and his bones ached from time to time, depending on the weather.

When the London drizzle was too constant, Mr. Baxter sat in a chair by the window. There were usually people in the street below, and the shop windows glowed with hope and promise. He knew each retailer by the sound of its bell, and there was a stand where two women sold flowers every day and on Saturday mornings, calling out to passersby in the style of East End market traders. Although Mr. Baxter had no interest in gardening, over time he had learned the Latin names of various plants, and sometimes caught himself saying them late at night when the street was empty.

At closing time, women came to vacuum the shops with chrome Hoovers. One of them was going to have a baby.

In the morning (after a few hours' sleep on the settee), Mr. Baxter normally drank his tea standing up at the window, as window cleaners sloshed down Jermyn Street with buckets and rags. Sometimes they whistled, and the sound fell from their mouths like silver thread.

If the weather was good enough for his daily walk in St. James's Park, Mr. Baxter often found an empty bench to rest and watch people go by, or clouds pass in lines of white shoulders. He wondered where everyone he saw was going, and stared at them the way an illiterate stares at words in a sentence.

There is a deep lake in the middle of St. James's Park, and Mr. Baxter often lingered there too, watching swans fold their wings, or women in head scarves toss crumbs from their pockets. He secured his coat at the waist by knotting a belt. It was a very old coat. Sometimes he wore it over his dressing gown to bed, and there were stains around the hem at the front where he had missed the toilet. He needed eyeglasses to see anything farther than his own large hands, and they were square with gold frames and a brown tint that was once fashionable. Sometimes, a flake of skin would lodge on the glass.

There *was* a time when Mr. Baxter was quite fashionable, and quite involved in goings-on around London—a regular face in the tabloids on account of his clients. But that was long ago, and so when he was woken up one night by someone shouting in the street, it was with more annoyance than concern that he untangled himself from the sheets, felt for his glasses, and shuffled quietly to the far window of the flat to see what was happening.

The person outside was screaming in Jamaican patois, as though involved in an argument, yet he appeared to be alone.

Just another teenage lout, Mr. Baxter thought, watching the boy pull at the matted clumps of his hair. It was midwinter, and puddles had hardened into ice. Mr. Baxter hoped he might slip on one.

After a while, he sat down and listened to the boy with both hands spread on the kitchen table as though he were a great pianist about to commence his magnum opus.

Of course, it would have been much quieter in the small bedroom at the back of Mr. Baxter's house, but for years he had slept every night on the settee. The expensive floral cotton sheets and pillowcases, purchased one summer afternoon on the top floor of Liberty, lay smooth and undisturbed, like an envelope sealed long ago with nothing inside.

WHEN THE SHOUTING man returned to Jermyn Street two nights later, Mr. Baxter listened from his pillow in a sort of daze. It was bitterly cold, and black taxis roared up the cobbled road, their heavy diesel engines rattling the windows.

This can't go on, Mr. Baxter thought. *I was in the middle of a bloody dream*. He folded back his sheets and perched on the edge of the settee. *All I'm asking for is a bit of peace, and now I've got some mad bastard out there.*

The pubs were still open, and the sound of people walking echoed through his apartment like disorderly music.

When Mr. Baxter unlatched the window and peered down at the figure, he noticed a plastic bag of clothes. The arm of a sweater reached out as if trying to escape. Mr. Baxter shook his head in reproach.

"Some people," he said loudly, "are a bleedin' nuisance!"

THEN FOR A week the man didn't come and Jermyn Street was a place of general quiet.

It was still so cold that the prime minister himself was telling people not to go out. The demand for coal and wood was unprecedented. Elderly people were found dead at home, upright in their chairs.

Mr. Baxter spent the week lying awake, wondering where the boy had gone, and whether he was inside or outside.

The night he returned, Mr. Baxter pulled on his dressing gown and hurried to the window. It was freezing, but the man below had neither gloves nor hat.

What an idiot, he thought. *His own bloody fault if he dies out there. Nothing to do with me.*

The few people who were out hurried home from the pubs in clouds of their own laughter. But then, a few shops away, Mr. Baxter heard bins being knocked over. In the distance, a woman and a man were struggling to walk a straight line; then the woman sat down in the middle of the road. The man pulled on her arm, which made her laugh and take a shoe off.

When a speeding car entered Jermyn Street, the boy below Mr. Baxter's window started shouting, "Check out *di rupshan!* Check out *di rupshan!*" Somehow understanding, the drunks lifted their heads and carried their bodies to the pavement, as the car roared past bound for lives less fortunate.

When the road was empty again, they resumed their stumble home through the darkness, and the young man went back to arguing with his imaginary foe.

As the kettle boiled, Mr. Baxter noticed a fork on the kitchen table, left there from his evening meal. Years ago, his father would sometimes wake him up very late at night, telling him to dress and come downstairs. He was only a child then, but understood it would have been worse not to go. Under his bed was a box of toy cars, a cricket bat, and a few broken Spitfire models he had been unable to complete on his own. Pinned to the wall was a football pennant he'd won at the seaside.

After going downstairs, Mr. Baxter would sit squarely in front of his father at the kitchen table, trying not to blink, and slowly hardening into the statue of a boy, so that when the fork came down on the backs of his hands repeatedly, he had only a vague feeling that parts of his body were cracking. Sometimes his father would laugh, or smash a bottle, or split a cupboard door with his elbow. Sometimes he would sweep everything out of the fridge and leave it on the floor.

The next morning, the teachers would want to know why Charlie Baxter couldn't hold his pencil—why his knuckles were black and yellow. He earned a reputation for having the hardest punch in school, though no one had ever seen him fight.

The teachers said the only thing worse than a big bully was a big liar, and made him stand in a corner until ready to confess. But to young Charlie Baxter, it was *their* special secret, and in his child mind, felt his father respected him for keeping it.

———

AFTER A WHILE, Mr. Baxter got tired and went back to the settee. It was warm under the blankets, and his bare feet felt good under the covers. He had no curtains, and moonlight washed over his things, pooling when furniture blocked its path. He thought about what had happened outside with the drunks and the speeding car, then, a moment before falling asleep, wondered if rage isn't just another form of crying.

In the morning, he cooked eight sausages, four eggs, a dozen mushrooms, an entire pack of bacon, and a whole can of Heinz Baked Beans, so that he could make a second, smaller breakfast plate, which he covered and put in the fridge.

Blackened morsels had stuck to the frying pan, but he persisted with the scouring pad, then hung the pan above the sink where it dripped onto a tea towel.

On his walk that day, Mr. Baxter noticed more birds than usual. They had congregated at one end of the pond, where park officials had broken the ice with heavy sticks. Then he stood for some time on the narrow bridge that stretched over the lake. On one side, up past the blowing bare trees and brown water, was Buckingham Palace; on the other side a slow rise of gray marble into Whitehall, where Union Jacks snapped in the wind. The view had not been altered for centuries, and for this reason the bridge was one of Mr. Baxter's favorite haunts, a place where he did not feel defined solely by the things he remembered.

THREE NIGHTS LATER, Mr. Baxter stirred a pot of tea and listened at the window. The moon was out and chalked the edges of a cold and frosty street.

Why hadn't someone called the police and reported a disturbance of the peace? It was now so irritating that Mr. Baxter wanted to aim his teapot at the man's head. He imagined going down there and stuffing him into his black bag of clothes, then tossing it into the icy Thames.

For the first time in years, Mr. Baxter felt violence bubbling to the surface of his life.

Then a bottle shattered against the wall of St. James's Church. Mr. Baxter looked out as another flashed past and landed silently on the boy's bag of clothes. Three men stormed across the road, fists spinning.

Mr. Baxter stood there shaking, his feet half in his slippers. He knew what was happening. He knew exactly what the men intended to do. And this confidence reminded him of who *he* was and of the things *he* had done. He stopped trembling, shuffled fully into his slippers, and tightened the string on his pajamas.

By the time he got down to the street, there were clothes everywhere, and the boy was a ball on the ground being kicked. The men were laughing and taking turns.

When the form of a giant appeared suddenly from a narrow door in the St. James's Church wall, wearing frayed gingham pajamas and enormous tweed slippers, the three men stopped what they were doing and just looked. For a moment, the sheer size of Mr. Baxter seemed to deter them. Then one came at him quickly with a broken bottle.

Mr. Baxter had grown up in the East End, and was once quite a dangerous man.

For several years he was Twiggy's bodyguard, then television celebrities, then private events, then nightclubs and well-known pubs in Sloane Square and Chelsea . . . .

He stopped working two decades ago, after waking up in the Royal Free Hospital.

"Who got me?" he said to the nurse. But it was painful even to chuckle.

"No one got you, Rambo," the nurse said. "You had a heart attack."

The next day, she brought flowers wrapped in pages from the *London Standard* and arranged them herself in the vase.

"I wouldn't waste those on me, darlin'," Mr. Baxter said.

"As these here are my flowers," the nurse told him, "I'll waste them on whomever I choose."

Some nights she stayed a bit later and read to him from a book.

No one had ever read to him from a book.

DOWN ON JERMYN Street, Mr. Baxter's body moved with the old knowledge. He was slower, but still mighty in his reach, and the man who had come at him with a bottle was soon on the ground with a shattered jaw. When a second attacker lunged, Mr. Baxter took a punch in the side of the head, then split the man's nose with a light jab and followed up with a hook. The third man just stood there screaming that he was going to stab Mr. Baxter—but then backed away when he noticed a figure running toward him up the street with an enormous pair of scissors.

When all three attackers had gone, the man on the ground tried to sit up. His face was an absolute mess. The tailor put down his garment scissors and breathlessly introduced himself as Colin. Then he pointed in the direction of his shop, "New and Lingwood, bespoke and ready-to-wear."

Mr. Baxter judged him to be about the same age as himself, but with a fuller head of hair and a faint South African accent.

"I'm Charlie Baxter."

"Yes, yes . . . I know who you are," Colin said, still trying to catch his breath in the freezing air. "The Menace of Mile End! I used to read about you in the papers years ago."

Then the man on the ground leaned on his hands and vomited.

Colin looked around at all the clothes. "I suppose we'd better pick these up," he said. "If you hand them to me, I'll fold them properly into the bag."

When they had finished, Mr. Baxter scooped the young man into his arms and carried him upstairs. Colin followed with the bag of clothes.

"MY GOODNESS," COLIN said as Mr. Baxter removed splinters of glass from the boy's face with a pair of tweezers. "What steady hands you have."

Then he watched as Mr. Baxter soaked an old paisley handkerchief in witch hazel and used it to disinfect the cuts and grazes.

———

WHEN THE KETTLE had boiled, they all sat together over mugs of tea until the windows glowed with first light. They also ate honey biscuits from Fortnum & Mason. On the tin, animals played musical instruments.

The young man didn't say much, but accepted each fresh cup of tea with both hands. He also kept looking to check that his bag of clothes hadn't moved from the hall.

After some consideration, Mr. Baxter thought the boy had a good face. *His profile was delicate, with high, almost regal cheekbones that captured light on their descent. And there was something pure about his eyes—something true and uncomplicated; something steady, which under the right circumstances could be lifted like a jewel from a crevice.*

. . . And it probably wouldn't cost the earth for Colin to knock him up a suit and some pajamas—give him something to do with that enormous pair of scissors he likes to wave about.

Before settling down on the settee for a few hours of sleep, it occurred to Mr. Baxter that the young man snoring in his back bedroom might wake up and kill him. *But then he's only a kid*, Mr. Baxter thought—*just a tired weight in an old man's arms—and there's something sacred about sleep, nature's way of saving us from ourselves.*

WHEN MR. BAXTER woke in the afternoon, it was clear that the young man had tried to make the bed before he left. It wasn't a bad job. The sheets were pulled up, but not even—and there were creases and dents, as though he had lain back down again.

After some toast and marmalade, Mr. Baxter stirred another pot of tea and looked out the window, past the old cheese shop and into New & Lingwood, where several mannequins gazed blindly into the street, their limbs divided with lines and numbers.

When Mr. Baxter went for his usual walk, he purposefully forgot his coat. Then, on his way back, he stopped into one of the less expensive men's outfitters on Jermyn Street and purchased a lovely full-length, double-breasted chesterfield with a velvet collar. When the tailor insisted he try it on, to prove it simply wasn't going to fit over his enormous frame, Mr. Baxter growled at him to stop meddling.

When he got home, he hung the coat on the back of the door. Then he made a cup of tea and looked at his hands, remembering how steady they'd been, removing the glass from the young man's face.

Then all the shops began to close.

Another day was almost over.

Men with briefcases and umbrellas hurried home to their wives and children. The radio said that snow was finally coming and that London would be thick with it by morning. Mr. Baxter imagined the hard cold broken into bright, falling pieces.

After listening to the six o'clock news on the BBC, Mr. Baxter tied on his apron and reached into the highest cupboard for a bag of flour. On his way home that day, he had also popped into Wiltons Restaurant to buy a couple of fish, but the chef seemed to know who he was and wouldn't take any money. Then at the small, bustling Tesco Metro Supermarket on the corner of Jermyn Street, Mr. Baxter had spent half an hour picking out the best Jersey potatoes, which he put in his basket with a pot of cream, a bunch of chives, and an onion. *The good thing about fish pie*, he thought, *is that it keeps.*

But somehow he knew it wouldn't go to waste, and as it bubbled in the bright, unbroken gaze of the oven, and the sky split in a fury of silent falling, Mr. Baxter opened every window in the house, for the great hunger that filled London was no longer his own.

The Goldfish

For Tinkerbell
2009–2013

AFTER LINING UP with a busload of schoolchildren, the old man bought a ticket and entered the aquarium through a pair of tinted glass doors.

For the first hour he drifted from room to room as if he were a fish himself, marveling at the different colors and shapes, and how some came right up to the glass.

Then a woman in overalls and white rubber boots emerged from a door marked STAFF ONLY. She was holding a bucket and there was tinsel tied around the handle because it was almost Christmas. The old man saw his chance.

"Excuse me, but is there someone I can talk to about fish?"

The woman stopped walking. "You can talk to me if you want."

"Oh good," said the old man, "Because I desperately need some help with Piper, my goldfish."

"I'm afraid we're not allowed to give advice to people who keep fish as pets."

"But it's only that Piper—"

"I'm sorry," the woman said. "I could lose my job."

——

A FEW DAYS later, the old man was scraping unsalted butter across a slice of toast when he overheard something on television about a new program called *Animal Hospital*.

Eureka! he thought, and went off in search of the Yellow Pages.

The next morning, he found himself sitting patiently in a crowded waiting room, flicking through a tattered magazine about hamsters.

When the old man signed in upon arrival, writing GOLD-FISH on the form, the receptionist said she'd talk to the doctor, but it was unlikely they'd be able to help.

After waiting almost an hour, a young man burst through double doors, his unfastened lab coat billowing like a cape. A few of the cats hissed.

The vet chatted with the receptionist for a few minutes, then looked into the sea of faces and signaled for the old man to come forward.

The bus ride home was miserable. The old man had felt certain that a trained animal doctor would have been able to help with Piper's condition. But then as the bus neared his stop and people stood to alight, the old man was struck dumb by the enlarged words of an advertisement on the back of someone's newspaper.

YOUR BEST FRIEND IS WAITING TO MEET YOU
AT GERALD'S PET PARADISE...

Below the slogan were cartoon pictures of dogs, cats, ferrets, and a smiling goldfish with bright teeth and long eyelashes. The old man strained to see, but without his glasses it was difficult to read. People pushed past, trying to get off the bus before the doors closed. When the driver told the old man he was blocking the exit, the woman lowered and folded her newspaper in one motion, then held it out.

"Take it," she said. "They're free."

The old man sat grinning in the bus shelter as he read the page over and over again. Soon, the failure of his afternoon had quite dissolved.

The shop was only a few streets away, and with Piper at home in extremis, the old man forced himself to stand and start walking briskly in the direction of Gerald's Pet Paradise.

When the last customer of the night burst in, Akin Okunadi, the young assistant, was playing a game on his phone, waiting for the owner to get back and close up for the night.

The old man looked around at all the colorful things for sale and, after regaining his composure, shuffled toward the counter past a stack of empty cages hung with miniature Christmas stockings.

When Akin saw the customer approach, he slipped the device into his pocket and asked if he could help.

"I would like to talk with somebody who knows about goldfish," the old man said.

"If it's food or filters, then I can help."

The old man looked Akin up and down. "I'm afraid it's more serious than that."

"You'd best wait for the manager then. He should be back in a minute. He deals with what's in the tanks."

"No, no, I'm not here to *buy* a goldfish," insisted the old man, "but to get some *advice* on one."

"Well, you'd better wait, because my only experience is when my brother got one at the fair."

"Oh, it's nice they still do that," the old man said buoyantly. "What did your brother name him?"

"He never got a chance. It died in the bag on the way home."

The old man looked at his shoes and said how very sorry he was.

"He only had it an hour," Akin laughed.

"An hour, a week, a decade," said the old man. "A fish is a fish."

Along the street, lights were going out one by one as shop-keepers closed up and went home for the night.

"I ain't seen you come in before, mister."

"That's because I get Piper's food and filters by mail order. I haven't needed a pet shop—until now, that is. I don't know why it didn't occur to me before."

Then he asked if Akin had heard anything about the snow-storm they were supposed to be having. The young assistant wondered if it would affect the bus service.

A few minutes later, the shop door swung open wildly.

"It's bloody raining!" Gerald shouted, not realizing they had a customer. "They always get it wrong, don't they?"

When he appeared from behind a rack of fake mice and rubber bones, he saw the old man standing at the counter.

"You must be the manager," the old man said.

"That's right, but I'm afraid we're closing in a few minutes."

"He's been waiting for you," Akin said. "Wants to ask your advice about his goldfish."

Gerald shot Akin a look of annoyance, then turned to the old man. "What is it, then? Food? Gravel? Tank toys?"

For a few moments the old man didn't move. Then, with a great show of emotion, heaved the words from his throat.

"My goldfish, Piper, has stopped moving."

Gerald nodded. "I see."

"He was first on his side—but now he's completely upside down."

"Is he dead?" Gerald asked.

The old man thought for a moment. "He's certainly very ill, gravely perhaps—but dead?"

"Well is he moving?"

"When I put my hand in the tank he moves. He bobs when I put my hand in and go like this." Gerald and Akin watched as the old man motioned in the air with his hand.

It was soon past closing and Akin would miss the 5:41 bus.

He lived with his mother and brother, Sam, who was ten years younger. Their house was half an hour across the city by bus. It had a small garden in the front that the wind filled with leaves and fast-food wrappers. The back garden—an uneven slab of concrete when they moved in—now had potted plants and a freestanding pond, where Akin and Sam sometimes arranged plastic soldiers on lily pads.

If it wasn't raining, Akin rode his old BMX to the pet shop. Their mother left early for work during the week, and so Akin made his brother's school lunches and saw him off. Their father had died while Akin's mother was in the hospital giving birth to Sam.

Sometimes Akin slipped notes into his brother's lunch box, lines from hip-hop tracks that were rude or funny. Sometimes his brother crept into his bed at night, then lay there in the darkness, his eyes completely open, thinking of questions and then forgetting them.

On the last Saturday of every month, Akin would take his brother into the city center to choose a new Xbox game. Their mother gave them money to have lunch and see a film. They pooled any change for comics, or a box of doughnuts, which they gobbled on the bus home.

GERALD EXPLAINED TO the old man that if his fish wasn't dead, it was probably constipated, and asked how often he cleaned the tank.

"Every Sunday," the old man said. "Like clockwork."

"In that case," Gerald instructed, "try feeding him frozen peas for a week."

The man fumbled in his coat pocket for a pencil and something to write on.

"How many peas exactly?"

"Two," Gerald said. "Take the skins off, then drop the bits in."

The old man jotted it down, then slipped the frayed envelope back into his coat pocket. "This is a great help, how much do I owe you?"

"Just five pounds."

The old man removed a large zip wallet, and from a mass of yellowing receipts located a five-pound note.

"Two peas a day, doctor's orders," said the old man, handing over the money.

"If it doesn't work, I've got freeze-dried fish laxative—but pea fragments are better if you can get them to eat it."

"Oh, I'll get him to eat it," the old man said firmly. "Before all this happened, he used to come right up to the glass whenever he saw me, just like those colorful fish at the aquarium."

Before leaving, the old man lingered in the shop doorway. Akin wondered if he wasn't going to say something about the unfair charge levied for advice.

"I know you want to close," the old man said, "but I have to ask—could it be anything worse than a digestive complaint?"

Gerald was straightening up a display of rubber Christmas trees. "Oh, absolutely—floating upside down could also be a bacterial infection or swim bladder disorder—in which case it's only a matter of time."

The old man didn't speak or move.

"You have to face facts," Gerald said. "Some fish just aren't going to make it."

It was twenty minutes before the next bus, so Akin decided to pick up a snack from the supermarket for his ride home. Browsing a selection of recently reduced items, he noticed a gray figure bending over a freezer.

"Hello," Akin said.

The old man looked up. "You're the lad from the pet shop."

"Buying peas for Piper?"

"That's right," said the old man. "But there's too much of a selection, I don't know which kind to get."

"Get organic ones."

"Are they better?"

"That's what my mum gives us."

Akin and the old man left the shop together and found themselves walking in the same direction. It was raining and neither had an umbrella.

When it began to pour, the old man asked Akin if he would like to come and meet Piper. His small pensioner's flat was only one street away, and there was an umbrella he'd be willing to lend the young assistant.

On the way there, Akin asked how long Piper had been upside down.

"About three weeks," the old man said. "He just hasn't been himself."

As they approached the concrete tower where the old man lived, Akin suddenly stopped.

"Oh no," he said, feeling his pockets. "I've forgotten my bus pass."

He knelt down and rummaged through his backpack.

"But we're here," the old man said, pointing to a sign that read GODWIN COURT. "This is where I live."

"Yeah, I know, but if I left my bus pass in the shop, I have to get it before Gerald closes up."

"Well, if you must go, I'm number three. I'll leave the door unlocked. You will come, won't you?"

THE RAIN TURNED to snow on Akin's journey back to the old man's apartment. Cars crawled along with their headlights burning.

There was a particular odor to 3 Godwin Court that Akin would forever associate with old age. Piles of newspapers rose up like small islands from a sea of carpet. Dirty clothes had been dumped in one corner, and in another, empty cereal boxes, egg cartons, and plastic ice cream containers with mold furring over the remains. The sink had not been touched for some time, and the standing water was coated by a dark skin. On the stove, unwashed pots and pans were piled up, most stained with corrosion or decaying food. A Victorian cabinet tucked into a corner of the sitting room was crowded with ceramic statues that looked out with delicate, painted eyes.

The fish tank was on a table next to a maroon armchair, and the old man was bending over it, fumbling with scissors and the bag of peas.

"They defrosted on the walk home," he said, "so I thought I might get the ball rolling. Piper is in here, if you want to come and meet him."

Akin stepped over to the tank and lifted the lid.

"Please be extra careful," the old man said. "As I told you, he's not well at all."

A large goldfish on the surface of the water was in the early stages of decomposition. Akin reached in and nudged the body with his finger.

"He never used to be so white," the old man said. "But I suspect that's just old age."

When Akin swirled the water, the goldfish bobbed in the sudden current.

"See how he moves when you put your hand in?" said the old man.

Akin cupped the fish in his hand and looked closely at its gills. "Hello," he whispered. "Can you hear me, Piper?"

After releasing the motionless body, Akin lowered the lid and washed his hands.

The old man was squeezing peas from their shells and lining them up on the counter.

"Two a day, I think your boss said. Shall we—"

"Before you do that, let's test the dopamine levels of the water."

The old man stopped what he was doing. "Dopamine levels?" he said incredulously. "What are they?"

"They're an indication of how clean everything is."

"Is it important?"

"Very. High levels of dopamine will lessen the healing qualities of each pea."

The old man just stood there. "I'm sorry now that I ever doubted your expertise."

"It's a test I recommend conducting at this stage," Akin went on. "But without my instruments, I'm going to need a piece of silver."

The old man thought for a moment. "Probably in the bedroom."

When he was out of sight, Akin took the tank lid completely off, then rummaged through his backpack for the container marked LIVE FISH that he had picked up on returning to the shop.

When he heard the old man coming back, Akin shouted that it was gold, and not silver he needed. The old man grunted and turned around. Akin poured the contents of the plastic container into the tank, then quietly put the lid back on.

"Will bronze work?" came a voice from the bedroom. Akin replied that bronze was even better, and the old man returned with the miniature statue of an elephant.

Akin told the old man to get more peas ready, then raised the tank lid and dipped the elephant's trunk in, just below the surface of the water.

The old man watched.

"Wow," Akin said. "These readings are hard to believe." Then he turned to the old man. "This water is so clean, the dopamine level ain't even registering."

"Scrubbed clean every Sunday," the old man assured him. "Rain or shine."

Akin tried to imagine how his mother might break it to the old man, if he were a child, like his younger brother, Sam.

"Before we go back to the peas," Akin said. "There's bad news and there's good news."

The old man's lower lip began to shake, and Akin could see how he might have looked as a boy.

"Which would you like first?" Akin asked. "Good news or bad news?"

The old man glanced at the cabinet of ceramic figures, then at the photographs on his mantelpiece, at faces once capable of moving and making sounds. They were people who had known him the way he remembered himself. The woman in the largest picture had been his wife. Sometimes it felt like she was just out shopping, or on the other side of a door about to come in.

"The good," he said finally. "because I'm an optimist at heart."

Akin took a deep breath.

"Well . . . the truth is—it wasn't constipation or Piper's bladder."

"Not his bladder?"

"Piper was pregnant."

For a few moments, the old man's expression did not change, as though words ceased to have any meaning.

"With twins," Akin said, pointing to two tiny new fish darting excitedly around the tank.

The old man moved his head as close to the glass as possible.

"Congratulations," Akin told him. "You're a grandfather."

The old man couldn't believe it. "All these years I thought Piper was a young chap!"

The tiny fish were unstoppable, flapping their bodies through the legs of a plastic deep-sea diver.

"And they've been in here all this time?"

Akin nodded.

"Tells you how bad my eyes are!"

When Akin explained that Piper had most likely died in childbirth some time ago, the old man had to sit down. Akin found some instant cocoa in the cupboard, then filled a kettle and bashed the cocoa with a spoon until it broke into chunks.

The old man went into detail about Piper as a young fish. Then he got up and stood over the tank, where his grandfish were scooting through Piper's old castle and fake plants.

"They're the spitting image of him," the old man said.

"And fish live longer when they have company."

When the reality of Piper's loss began to sink in, Akin put his hand on the old man's shoulder. "Loads of fish die in childbirth," he said. "It's a lot of stress for them to push the fish babies out."

"But, what I don't quite understand," said the old man, turning to Akin, "is how Piper got in the family way to begin with?"

"Well," Akin said, trying to think of something, "I suppose it's like Mary and the baby Jesus."

"The Bible story?"

"Yeah, but underwater."

The old man thought about it.

"My wife, Doris, and I never had any children ourselves. I got Piper after she died just to have a little friend in the house."

"Now you've got two little friends."

THE OLD MAN wanted to lift Piper's body out by himself but couldn't steady his hands, so Akin took the spoon from him. It wasn't the first time something like this had happened.

When Akin was nine years old, he came home from school and found his father in the upstairs bathroom on the floor with a plastic bag over his head. Akin tried to get the bag off, but there was too much tape and his fingers kept slipping.

Sometimes he dreamed that it was happening again, and sometimes the bag came off and he saw his father's eyes.

THE OLD MAN watched as Akin scooped up Piper's body in the spoon.

"Dear God," Akin said. "Please accept Piper into your flock in Heaven."

Akin offered to take Piper's body to the park, but the old man said he'd bury her in the morning under one of his potted plants.

Akin put the kettle on again and watched the old man sprinkle a few meal flakes for the two young fish, who were zooming around in the water, completely unaware of the tragedy from which their lives had sprung forth.

While they were on the couch holding mugs, the old man said he was going to call one of Piper's children Akin, if Akin didn't mind.

"Call the other one Doris," Akin said.

———

IT TOOK A long time to get home. The bus was crowded with people talking about the snow, and there were several text messages from his mother, asking where he was.

As Akin neared the front door of his house, he noticed light falling from the living room window onto a patch of shallow snow. He stepped over and put his face to the glass. His mother and brother were on the sofa and didn't see him. The television was on and the night echoed with the faint ring of applause. His brother's feet were on a cushion and his mother was rubbing them with an expression Akin recognized as worry. There were empty choc-ice wrappers on the arm of the sofa, and a loose stack of Chinese takeaway containers on the carpet.

In the far corner of the living room was a Christmas tree. It was tall and well lit. They bought it from an all-night convenience store that kept them outside between bundles of firewood and boxes of vegetables.

Sam insisted on carrying one end of the tree, but had to keep stopping to rest.

When they got home, their mother kicked off her slippers to climb the attic ladder and get the Christmas things down. Akin waited on the second step for her to lower the boxes.

They spent the afternoon decorating the tree with ornaments that caught the light. As they were putting the star on, Sam asked if Santa Claus was real.

"Of course he is!" their mother exclaimed. "Haven't you made your list yet?"

After she had vacuumed up the needles, they held hands and cheered when the lights came on.

Sam lay on his back and looked up into the branches.

On the mantelpiece were photographs from their summer holiday in Cornwall.

One night they couldn't find a bed-and-breakfast and had to sleep in the car. Sam said if anyone came he'd protect them, though Akin knew it would be up to him as the older brother, and stayed awake as long as he could, waiting for figures beyond the glass to bear down upon them. But all he saw was the faint glow of stars from deep in the universe; proof that other worlds are as imaginary as this one.

A Slow and Deliberate Disappearance

THE MAGICIAN ARRIVED in a small gold car, then changed in the men's restroom. He wore makeup and a dinner jacket with a tear in the breast pocket.

Lights had been on throughout the facility since lunchtime. Rain lashed the windows. Everything in the garden was blowing around, and fallen leaves made the paths slippery. It was late autumn and the days were shorter.

The magician asked everyone's name. His finger swung from face to face, but only half the group answered. Some couldn't remember, while others had lost the ability to speak and be understood. The nurses didn't intervene. They perched on stools between wheelchairs and were always calm. Residents on the chintz sofa looked small or twisted.

The magician's name was Eric and his first trick involved a slow and deliberate disappearance.

His own children, who were in high school, often made fun of him. They smoked pot and didn't always show up when it was his day to see them. Eric had been out of full-time work most of his life. Card tricks and disappearing balls were only a hobby, but they paid enough to cover rent and gas. Any tips were saved for movie tickets or the latest video game he heard teenagers were lining up to get.

Eric's wife had divorced him three years ago.

She was from San Antonio. The night they met, she was wearing tight jeans and cowboy boots. Eric kept buying drinks and they played pool. He remembered that night like a music video. They were married within a year. Her sister and mother came up from Texas. She insisted on a white wedding, and their first dance was to something quick by Garth Brooks.

Eric worked then at Carpet Warehouse. But the dry, chemical smell of dyed fabric made him sneeze, so he left that job for another, stacking shelves at a discount supermarket. But the manager said he was too slow *facing out* and mixed things up in the warehouse.

When his wife got home from work, she would take off her shoes and drink wine. Eric looked forward to them watching *The Late Movie*, and muted the commercials so she could talk about her day. He didn't mind not having a job, and wrote himself out a routine for cleaning, tidying up, and laundry that he put on the refrigerator for his wife to see.

At least he was there when the kids got home, to fix snacks and to play. Also, he learned the correct times to cook anything from frozen, and served grilled-cheese sandwiches by sliding each stack dramatically from a sizzling pan onto plates like a Benihana chef.

But after ten years like this everything changed.

The children had grown private and liked to stay in their rooms. His wife began working longer hours and going out with her colleagues on weekends. Eric stuck to the routine as much as possible—staying up for *The Late Movie*, doing laundry on

Wednesday and Friday, and practicing his magic after meals once the table had been cleared.

Then, one Saturday morning, as Eric was changing a light-bulb in the refrigerator, his wife came to him very upset and said she wanted a different life—one she had been imagining. He followed her upstairs and sat on a corner of the bed. She told him their marriage was at an end and she wanted to separate. The television was on downstairs. Eric could hear the kids laughing. His wife said she would take the children to the mall that afternoon and explain what was happening.

He was to pack a bag and go before they got back. The next day, she would run errands so Eric could see his kids for a few hours. This would be the first of his allowed visitations, she said.

The house was in her name and they would share custody.

As he was still unemployed, she would not ask for alimony.

She had never seen a man cry in such a way, and tried to comfort him by saying that the children didn't need looking after anymore. In a few years they would be out of school and have their own lives.

For six months, Eric lived at the Best Eastern Motel in Union City. He used to sleep with the curtains open because the sign, lit up at night, made him think of Las Vegas.

Then he found an apartment near the golf course.

He had taken a few things from the house but didn't want to upset his kids' sense of order. There was a wooden bed already in the apartment when he moved in. It had E.T. stickers on the headboard and they glowed in the dark. He used to lie there looking at E.T.'s glowing finger, wondering if there really were other worlds and if he would ever see one.

A year later at a yard sale, he picked up a couch and a circular table where he could eat dinner and practice new tricks.

Eric had always believed that magic was his chance to do something great, and he dreamed of performing at luxury hotels and casinos for honeymooners and conference executives. It was one of the few things his kids still loved to see—even if they no longer believed that magic was real.

A FEW OF the residents clapped after each trick, copying the nurses. When the cards came out, the magician asked for a volunteer to shuffle, but then thought worse of it. If the deck fell, the few who *were* watching might start to give up.

Then a resident raised her hand. When Eric approached with the cards, she pointed to the man next to her. "Bill's good at this," she said.

Bill nodded and reached for the deck.

The magician felt renewed by their confidence and watched the cards flutter in the old man's hands like an accordion.

"That's good," the magician said. "Great handwork, Bill."

"He also plays the piano," the woman added. "Sometimes I think it's the radio, but it's him!"

Bill handed the cards back. The magic act continued with scatterings of applause.

The final trick involved a hat and silk handkerchiefs.

A nurse with braces on her teeth seemed especially interested, so the magician asked her to step forward and hold the squares of silk that kept appearing from the hat.

It was almost time for supper. Everything was ready and the

cooks stood with their arms folded. The kitchen staff watched too, setting down silverware as quietly as possible.

The nurse holding the silk squares remembered setting the table as a little girl. Her name was Mary Ann. She'd grown up on a street with other Italians. Her brother joined the Air Force, and had a box of Star Wars figurines under his bed, which he looked at whenever he came home. Their late grandmother's station wagon was still in the driveway. Its blue fabric roof was ripped and it didn't run. Sometimes her father sat in it with the cordless phone and made bets.

Mary Ann went to see them as much as she could. Her father read the paper and her mother cut out coupons she'd never use, telling her all the people she knew who were getting divorced.

The family dinner plates had pictures and a faded gold rim. Her parents had received them as a wedding gift. Each bite revealed part of the picture. On one plate, a cart was being pulled through a low river. Children on the riverbank rubbed their hands. The sacks on the cart bulged like full stomachs. There was also a dog, and the horses moved slowly. The children in the picture didn't have shoes and could play all day. Mary Ann was grown up now, but the children on the dinner plates were still children.

Once, on a school trip to the city museum, Mary Ann had seen the same picture hanging in a gallery with its own security guard.

The smallness of their lives frightened her.

THE MAGICIAN BROUGHT his show to a close. Outside, it was still pouring. When a series of flashes made the lights flicker, a few of the residents suddenly clapped. Thunder made the dinner glasses ring.

Bill the card shuffler, pianist, and longtime resident had once been in a storm that kept him and his wife another night at a motel in Union City. There was a mustard-colored telephone, a pack of cards, and a Bible in the bedside table.

Bill's wife made him roll off her stockings. Then she lay back and reached out her arms. Her hair was still wet from the bathwater. A gold necklace lay flat upon her chest. Their kisses were quick and hot.

After, they smoked in bed. Bill held the ashtray. There was also some gin in the car, and she watched from the window as Bill searched the trunk in the pouring rain. They were tired but couldn't sleep. Bill had taken the hotel cards and shuffled them into equal stacks for a game.

All that remained of his marriage now, the only evidence of a grand family home, had been distilled into the few possessions that decorated his room at the facility: a New England writing desk, a brass lamp, and a lone dining chair that stood beside his electric hospital bed, along with the gray machine that would one day keep him alive.

When she was training as a nurse, Mary Ann learned that the worst comes when the body goes dumb. At night she and others worked quickly and quietly, wiping and drying, rubbing in creams with an odor that lingered on her hands and carried into her other life.

After the magic show, the nurses told Bill how well he had shuffled the magician's deck. The woman sitting next to him who had been kind was called Wilma. She referred to him as "my Bill," and got upset when anyone else sat beside him in the Nutmeg Room for meals.

Bill's face had once been full and dark. The nurses called him Cary Grant. They guessed what he was like in his heyday. A trench coat. Umbrella. Aftershave. Newspaper folded under one arm. They imagined him dancing. Opening doors for women. Eating cherry pie at lunch counters in a three-piece suit. They looked at the things in his room when he was asleep—fingered the Wedgwood cuff links he kept in a motel ashtray.

Wilma had once been a physician, but could no longer apply even a Band-Aid by herself. She had the notion of once being a mother, but couldn't be sure whether it was a boy or a girl. *Any* visitor could have been her child.

On summer afternoons, Bill and Wilma sometimes pored over a jigsaw before dinner, or sat outside on a bench with their bodies touching, dusk settling on tall trees.

Bill had been admitted to full-time care after taking a taxi to work one day, seventeen years after his retirement party. His wife consulted their daughter in Seattle, and they agreed that care was the right thing. Bill's wife wasn't allowed to stay with him in the home—even on the first night—but all Bill cared about was finding his slippers.

Wilma was in a terrible state when, years later, she was admitted to the center. She had been leaving things on. Going out in winter without a coat. Looking frantically for a dog that had died years before.

Of course, Bill had been through it all. Aging is not for sissies! he told her.

———

Eric was invited to stay for dinner after the show. Entertainers were always seated at a top table and asked to wear a red hat that identified them. He talked about magic and did the table tricks his kids liked to see growing up.

When they were in middle school, Eric's children had loved to watch wrestling on TV—so much that Eric found a place where they could see it live. Afterward, the wrestlers came out, and the kids lined up to get T-shirts signed. The concession stand sold cardboard photos of wrestlers in their costumes. On the train home they ate doughnut holes and argued about which wrestler was the nicest in real life.

One time, a drunk guy stumbled into their train car. He was not wearing any shoes. When he overheard what they were talking about, he told Eric's kids that wrestling was fake. When he tried to grab one of the cardboard pictures, Eric whipped out his fake thumb and made a five-dollar bill disappear. The drunk moved closer. Eric's children had seen it before, but watched as though it were the first time. Then the drunk man said that he wanted to try, and Eric took his hand at the wrist and taught him the correct motion.

Mary Ann brought the magician his dinner on a tray. Prime rib au jus with baby carrots and a dinner roll. When Eric asked for a beer, she laughed and sat beside him.

Eric wanted to know about the man who had shuffled the cards and the woman who volunteered him.

Other nurses chimed in.

"Bill centers her," one of them said.

"And when she goes, the other won't be long after," said another.

Wilma sometimes kept the things Bill gave her. She had them under her pillow and put her hands on them at night. His room was at the other end of the hall, and she imagined him, younger but in the same pajamas, eyeglasses on the edge of his nose, a ribbon of brandy on the bedside table, the street outside gleaming with old and heavy cars.

She wondered if he had been faithful.

She knew he was married because he still wore a ring.

If Bill had any kids, they had given up, because no one came.

A few times a year a woman appeared and said she was Wilma's daughter. She spent time with Bill too, holding his hand so he wouldn't feel left out.

Wilma felt she was a nice person and obviously meant well, but what a relief when she left in the evening; it took so much effort to pretend. Wilma's memories were more foreign to her now than dreams, and the world outside, a place where she had already ceased to exist.

Bill's lips reassured her whenever he spoke. There was something noble and magnanimous in their shape that seemed to forgive the world for letting them get old. Wilma imagined lying upon them, and a moment before sleep, plunging weightless into the darkness of his mouth—into everything he wanted to tell her.

Sometimes Wilma remembered random things, such as her driveway, and the feeling of pulling into it with a bump. Or was it the house where she grew up and her father was driving?

Now and then, she heard a dog bark.

"Where's the dog?" she once asked Bill. "I haven't fed the dog."

Bill told her not to worry—that the dog was in Heaven.

"A puppy again, Bill?" Wilma had answered, hopefully.

He had a dog too. Sometimes he felt the sensation of his hands in its yellow coat.

Usually in the afternoon, the nurses put opera on a headset for Bill, which made it impossible for Wilma to talk, so she went to her room and slid into bed.

She once remembered that her own husband loved the operatic works of Henry Purcell—and she told Bill about her engagement during a New Year's Eve performance of *Dido and Aeneas*. She did it to make him jealous, but he only went quiet, and wouldn't talk to her until he forgot that he wasn't talking to her, and everything was fine again.

Bill had been married too, but couldn't even remember the small, trivial things that sometimes came to Wilma. He knew more about the nurses' lives than he did his own. Not long after arriving at the facility, Bill had dumped his family photo albums in the trash. Got tired of wondering who they all were.

BEFORE LEAVING, ERIC went up to the nurse who had sat next to him and asked if she might have a meal with him next week.

Men looked at her sometimes at red lights, but in the bars only married guys seemed interested. It had been a long time since her last date. His name was Vincent and they went to an Italian place and ate eggplant. He owned a beer distributor and was saving up for a boat.

The manager of the facility thanked the magician and gave

him a check for three hundred dollars. Eric held it up and said he would go home and make another one appear.

At the door, he told Mary Ann that he hoped to see her again. Then, for some reason, he thought of the old man who had shuffled the cards.

"Must be nice," he said. "For an old man like that to have such a good friend as that woman."

Mary Ann laughed and looked at her white nurse's shoes.

"I'll tell you a secret," she said. "Bill and Wilma have been married for almost sixty years—but think they met here."

The Muse

IT WAS ALMOST midnight when her flight landed.

Outside the terminal, taxi drivers drank coffee to keep themselves awake until morning. Being together helped pass the time. It reminded Alexandra of the men from her Ukrainian village who drove the school buses. How they clustered in the playground near the swings, waiting for the last bell that would summon everyone home to bright kitchens with extended family visiting from Kiev or Lutsk.

Alexandra used to watch the bus drivers through her classroom window, laughing and chattering and moving their feet to keep warm. *The children we once were,* she thought, *live inside us like rings on a tree.*

On her way from the airport to the hotel, the driver asked if she was thirsty, or would like the radio turned on. It had been raining all day, he told her. Then at dusk the rain stopped and there were people on the street again.

Alexandra sometimes sent postcards to her parents in Sernyky, but never went beyond a description of the weather or some trivial detail of place. There were always more feelings than words to describe them.

The car was warm and quiet. There was a beige cashmere blanket on the backseat. Alexandra put it behind her neck as a pillow. The city was illuminated entirely by streetlight and the bright shop windows made her feel safe. She imagined people in their homes, watching television, or sitting in bed, or eating something. Children had already swum out to sleep; bedroom doors left ajar kept their lives within reach.

The driver asked if she was hungry. When she said she wasn't, he asked if she had come a long way.

Three or four times a year, Alexandra vanished like this, from her public world as a fashion designer to a city where she had no fixed identity.

We're not who we think we are, nor how others see us . . . , she once wrote in her journal. *Long before death, we die a thousand times at the hands of definition. . . .*

After being alone for a few days, she would feel some pull of inspiration. It could come from anywhere: lemons in a bowl were enough; the blowing trees in the park were enough; the migration of clouds; the color of water; words from a passing conversation she carried with her like loose stones. From such feelings, Alexandra would create things for people to wear.

WHEN THEY ARRIVED at the hotel, somebody opened her door. Her luggage was a single trunk with two initials on the outside. The receptionist wore silver-framed glasses and a light coating of aftershave. He said his name was Robert. His hair was thin and combed neatly to one side. He was happy to see her. The concierge on duty had been tracking her flight, and the mannequins and fabrics had arrived early from Milan and were in her suite as requested, as were several vases of her favorite white flowers.

Alexandra signed the guest register and asked Robert if he had long before he could go home.

"When the streetlights go off," he said, "I know it's almost time." He told her that he didn't mind being up late, and looked forward to eating breakfast with his partner before he left for his own job.

Each new collection began like this, in a city with no association. Alexandra would wander the streets, stroll through a bustling market, ride an empty bus—drink coffee in a dockside café as birds circled the open mouth of dawn.

In Berlin two years ago, Alexandra found a bench in the Volkspark Friedrichshain and watched people walk in circles, as though winding up the city.

Then she found Uhrenwerkstatt, a shop that repaired watches and clocks. She went in and asked the owner to show her all the pieces no one had come back for. At first he was reluctant, but then, with a dozen timepieces laid out on a cloth, he couldn't stop talking.

Her winter collection that year was called *Zeit Verloren* or *Time Lost*.

WHEN HER TRUNK was wheeled away on a lobby cart, Robert told the concierge he was leaving the desk—but then a telephone rang and Alexandra said quickly that she was fine, and wanted to go up to her room alone.

As she stepped across the marble floor toward a bank of hotel elevators, she noticed a man standing very still with his eyes closed. He was holding a loose manuscript under one arm and his hands were in his pockets.

"Excuse me," she said, noticing something by his shoe. Alexandra bent down and picked it up. "I think you've lost a button."

The man opened his eyes and stared at her.

"Let me sew it on for you."

"No, no, that's all right," he said, feeling for the errant thread on his velvet jacket. "I'm sure I can do it myself. How hard can it be?"

"Harder than you think. Come on."

She led him over to the lounge and reached into her pocket for the silver sewing kit she always carried. It had belonged to her grandmother, and was the only thing she was afraid of losing.

As he was removing his jacket, Alexandra noticed two stone statues behind him in the lobby. She imagined fingers shaping the cool rock, the pressure required to round a cheek or straighten a nose. The possibility of an expression, but the impossibility of breath.

She was tired from her flight, and it took time for her fingers to thread the needle and position the button.

"I hope I didn't disturb you," she said. "You were standing there with such concentration."

The man moved slightly in his seat. "I was thinking about that chandelier," he said, pointing. "I'm here to finish a screenplay and I've decided the chandelier is somehow a part of it. I usually write in the lobby at night, then sleep in the day."

"Why not work in your room," Alexandra asked, "where it's quiet?"

The man set his manuscript down on the seat and considered her question. "Maybe, in order to make people up, I need to see real ones."

Alexandra glanced up from her task. "Your chandelier reminds me of the heavy snows we had in Ukraine when I was a girl. But I don't suppose you know where that is. Most people don't."

The man turned to look. "Oh, I know exactly where it is," he said.

"Please don't say Russia. . . ."

The man smiled to show he understood, but kept staring past her at the chandelier. "Amazing how you see only the shape of light and not the material it's made from. Inspiration has assumed the form."

"Sounds like something a writer would say," Alexandra said. "Very artsy."

The man laughed. "I was raised to think that art was God's work. My adoptive family was quite religious. Southern Baptists. Very strict."

"You were adopted?"

"As a baby."

When she'd finished, Alexandra tugged at the button, then gave the man his jacket.

"It was kind of you to do this."

"Blame my grandmother."

After he went upstairs, Alexandra decided to stay in the lounge and have tea by the fire. Robert was still at the check-in desk, and she watched him pick up the phone, nod, and write things down. She imagined him driving home through the cool morning air. The sound of his key churning the lock. Dawn pouring into the dark house. His partner stirring in the bed they have shared for so long. His head on the pillow. She wondered if Robert ever just stood there, watching him sleep.

Later on, as she was settling into her room, there was a gentle knock.

It was the concierge. "I'm sorry to bother you so late," he said, handing her a sheaf of loose papers. "But the waiter found this where you were sitting downstairs."

After he had gone, she read a few lines. It was a film script. On the second page it said:

> *Dedicated to God.*
> But if God doesn't exist,
> Then to Larry.

When she was ready for bed, Alexandra got under the covers and continued reading.

IN THE MORNING, she drank black coffee and looked out the window. It was very early. She peered out over the rooftops and imagined each tall building slowly filling with people. A thousand days would soon begin—each one different from the other and impossible to predict. The sky above a single mass of white.

Alexandra loved the severity of hotel sheets, and wondered how many feathers were stuffed inside her pillows, and what a shame they were no longer in the sky, attached to birds.

After another cup of coffee, she began to draw.

With a Japanese fountain pen and a bottle of engraver's ink, she made sketches of the vague figures she had seen in her dream, and then of the landscape beyond her window, the seagulls, puffs of smoke, even the motionless animation of the lobby chandelier, which had so compelled the man downstairs that he made it a character in the ending of his screenplay.

Untitled by Michael Snow was a love story, but to Alexandra it lacked some vital element, like each of the characters in *The Wizard of Oz*. It was not an *ending* he needed, but a pulse that beat independently of its creator.

She ate some breakfast, then found her sunglasses and tied on a silk scarf. Before leaving her room, she called the front desk and was transferred to the room of Michael Snow. She wondered if he wrote under a pseudonym, but then realized that every name is a pseudonym. *Language merely points*, she had read once in a book of German poetry; *the rest must be imagined.*

When no one answered, she left a message, explaining what had happened with his manuscript being left downstairs, that she had to go out—but to meet her by the pool around four P.M.

SOMETIME IN THE afternoon, after a full day of walking around, Alexandra returned to the silence of her suite. It was a comfort to come back, as though part of her had stayed in the room.

She removed her scarf and sunglasses and flicked on the lamp. From brown paper, Alexandra unwrapped an artist's marionette she had bought at a shop with paper boats in the window. She set it on the desk and stared at the blank expression. Just like the statues downstairs in the lobby, it was a face that would never feel disappointment, nor flush with desire; no breath within its cheeks would ever quicken with the anticipation of being touched; it was in a human shape but lacked all humanity. She judged it to be interesting because it made her feel things that were missing. And that was the problem with Michael Snow's screenplay, she realized, seeing the manuscript on her desk—that it worked so hard to conjure love, when love was most felt in its absence.

THE LIFEGUARD FOLLOWED her silent path through the water. Light falling through the conservatory glass made her body look porcelain, and the opaque blue waves of the pool and the echo of people whispering made Alexandra feel like some doomed heroine from a 1920s novel.

Nearby, a couple was reading from the same copy of the *Wall Street Journal*. Their voices hovered over the blue water. The woman had tied up her hair in the style of a ballerina.

Outside the hotel, trees bent as the wind took their leaves.

When it was almost four o'clock, Alexandra realized that she'd left the man's script in her suite. By the time she returned to the pool, its author had arrived and was in the water. Alexandra watched his arms open and close. He seemed uncertain, and she suspected a childhood far from the sea or from some great river, like the Styr, which flowed only a few miles west of her village.

She waved, then sat down and flicked through the screenplay with a pencil.

The first thing she did was cross out *Untitled* on the first page, and write: *The story of love is also the story of loneliness?*

After a few laps, the man got out and dried his body with a towel. Then he put on a robe, and came over.

The waiter noticed she had company and brought menus.

"I'm afraid there are no chandeliers in here to inspire you," Alexandra said when he sat down. "Just a cocktail menu."

He saw she had written things on his script, but instead asked about her morning in the city. Had she seen the museum? The path around the lake? The little shops in the arcade?

She gave a few details, then asked about his life growing up in America.

He described things he thought might interest her, like going to revival, and church camp, and vintage car shows, and the annual state fair with country music stars sculpted from butter.

Alexandra tried to imagine it all, tried to conjure a picture of him with friends in a Chevy or a Ford, opening all the windows, screaming the way Americans did in films when they were happy, singing along to the radio, the excitement of being out late, the glory of a night sky under which everything in the history of the world had once happened, and was now happening to him.

He could not have known then, she thought, *how one day he would live his life somewhere else—and that his happiness would come from things he had no notion of then, and from people he did not know even existed.*

He told the story of his first script and the long drive to Los Angeles in a half-ton white pickup truck. When he arrived, they wouldn't even let him through the studio gates to deliver it. The guard said it happened every day.

He found a two-room apartment in Echo Park and called his family once a week. He sold his truck to a contractor in Venice and bought an English motorcycle with a kick start. He said that

Los Angeles was full of secular zeal, and that he often wrote in a booth at the twenty-four-hour kosher deli on Sunset Boulevard.

One night he made friends with an elderly man in a tweed cap who used to come in for soup and just sit there. The old man was a writer too. He had worked with James Dean early in his career, and won an Oscar for Best Picture. After a while they began sitting in the same booth. One of the first things Larry told him was that you don't write stories—they write you.

Larry lived in Pacific Palisades, but had been raised in Brooklyn by Orthodox Jewish parents from Ukraine.

Over the next couple of years, Michael and Larry discussed many things—not only whether God existed and differences between Judaism and Christianity, but ethics, beauty, theories of the universe, baseball, wives and marriage, the origins of war. Larry said he dreamed of going to Ukraine, literally dreamed of it: walking through fields barefoot at sunset . . . the impulse to pray *Ma'ariv* . . . his mother's hands, and how they seemed to get smaller and smaller, until only the memory of how they felt remained.

One day Michael had the idea to write a screenplay about the Old Testament story of Abraham and his son Isaac—a movie set in the present day, about parents willing to sacrifice the life of a child for their belief in some greater good. Larry helped Michael draw in the scenes, trim the dialogue, use silence effectively. . . .

Six months later, a big studio bought the script and began casting.

ALEXANDRA SAID THAT Larry sounded a little like her own father, with whom she would go walking or fishing. She described the place where she grew up in Ukraine, the snowfall, and the narrow lanes along the border with Belarus, the cool shade of trees in summer, and the dry, incessant wind.

When she told him the name of her fashion house, Michael admitted that he'd heard of it—had read about her in newspapers, even passed one of her boutiques on Melrose Avenue—but to him she was just a woman who had kindly sewn on his button the night before.

She confessed how it felt to see people wearing the dresses she designed: how it made her shy, how she hoped each piece enabled some secret part of the self to be shared with the world. And designing for runway was exhausting, she said, the traveling endless.

When she was a girl her family had taken their meals at a large table—though not always at the same time. Sometimes she sat watching her mother boil pans of water for vegetables and large cuts of meat. Sometimes she wrote her name in steam on the window, then peered through each letter into winter's heart. On cold Sunday afternoons, she went with her father to the shed for logs. They were stacked under a blue tarp. He wrapped the pieces she was to carry in an old blanket to prevent splinters. Once a month her mother spread a towel on her shoulders, then the tug of wet hair and the small, ensuing snips of her hairdresser's scissors; her mother shaking the towel over the sink, then the knock of a broom under the seat.

Her grandmother watched from the kitchen table.

"*She* was religious," Alexandra said. "But not like you— more like Larry. They would have had things in common, I'm sure, like special words and customs, how things are supposed to be done. That's all lost to me, I'm afraid, I don't even celebrate the holidays. . . ."

Michael listened as other moments of childhood rose to the surface of her eyes.

When he asked what inspired her to become a designer, she told him how, one night when she was little, she'd woken up and wandered into the kitchen because her throat was dry.

Sitting in the half-dark was her grandmother. She was repairing some garment with a needle and thread, and had not heard the figure of a child approach from behind. Alexandra remembers her sitting there, very still, in a deep chair beside a table of family photographs.

Some of the pictures showed her late husband, and the many ages they had lived through. On her grandmother's lap was the wool jacket he wore when they were young and took weekend trips in a silver car to Kiev. She was mending a tear in the lining, and with each loop, fused the separated pieces of fabric into one piece.

In a wicker basket by her foot were other items that belonged to the family, including one of Alexandra's bears, which was missing an eye.

It was the first of many nights when she would creep out of bed and listen to her grandmother's quiet hands working. Sometimes she would mutter something, or cease her sewing as winter flakes brushed the window.

Not long after, she died in her favorite chair, which Alexandra's father used to carry outside when she wanted the sun on her cheeks. They all thought she was sleeping.

Going through her things after the funeral, Alexandra's mother discovered a small box under the old woman's bed. It contained silver needles, thimbles, old spools, scissors, and a note addressed to her granddaughter.

Олександра,

Спасибі за мені компанію на тих довгих ночей.

Я хочу, щоб ви це швейний набір.

Тепер ви будете знати, свою владу.

бабуся*

ALEXANDRA DINED LATE in her suite listening to the faint applause of rain upon the window. It was Sunday night in a foreign city.

She cut wide patterns of fabric from the rolls of cloth and pinned them to her mannequins, folding and layering each piece instinctively.

About midnight she put away the fabric and went downstairs with her sketchbook.

As expected, Michael was writing quietly in the lobby. He was surprised to see her, and thanked her again for making notes on his script and for their talk at the pool.

She sat directly across from him, and for hours they worked together in silence, her hand moving of its own accord, making one sketch after another.

When she began to feel tired, her strokes grew slower and more deliberate.

Then, when her eyes closed, her head fell slightly to one side, as though tipping the last of her thoughts onto the page.

Michael stopped what he was doing and looked at her hands, remembering how they had sewn on his button the night before.

---

* *Thank you for keeping me company on those long nights.*
I want you to have this sewing kit.
By now you will know its power.

Then he moved carefully toward her, the way he imagined she had moved so as not to disrupt the rhythm of her grandmother's sewing. In her face, Michael saw the expression of the child who had stood there in the darkness, and the heavy, rolling flakes of snow that behind the veil of her sleep were still falling.

Before she could wake up, he took from his pocket the tiny Star of David necklace left behind by his friend, which he knew had traveled vast distances and borne witness to many things. Alexandra's pocketbook was open on the floor and he dropped it in without any sound.

On the flight home to Los Angeles, he wondered if one day she would find it—turn it over in her fingers, as if trying to connect the chain and silver points to a memory. But if such a thing didn't happen it wouldn't matter, for he would never again have to worry that what had been given up, was also lost.

Infidelity

MICHAEL AND JUDY had sushi that night because their mother and father were leaving for Los Angeles. The restaurant was near their apartment in the Williamsburg section of Brooklyn. Michael wanted noodle soup with a fried egg on top. Judy had a California roll. The waiter brought tea and small cups without handles. Judy kept looking at her phone until her mother said something.

After the meal, they got up and put their coats on to leave. Michael took the striped candy that came with the check and unwrapped one for his older sister.

The sidewalk was busy with people coming from the subway on North Seventh Street. Michael raised the hood of his jacket against the wind. It was spring, but the weather was yet to turn. The headlights of cars on the cold street made him reach for his mother's hand. They would soon be home, and he could go into his bedroom and lie on the floor, or play video games, or look at his fish and tap the glass. Then his mother stopped walking because Judy was lagging behind.

"C'mon, Judy," Rebecca called. "Please stop texting and do up your coat."

The weekend before, Rebecca had taken her to Bergdorf Goodman to pick out a new coat for spring. They selected a few possibilities, then lunched on the eighth floor, where the waiters wear green knit ties. Outside the restaurant, currents of people drifted along Central Park South, past the Plaza and the horsemen in top hats offering rides to young families and couples. They had once taken a loop around the park in a carriage, but Judy could hardly remember it now.

Over lunch, Rebecca noticed Judy watching a table of girls just a few years older than she. The girls had expensive pocketbooks and kept covering their mouths to laugh. When dessert came, Judy asked loudly for a macchiato, and Rebecca remembered enough about being young to say nothing.

After lunch, they went downstairs to make a final decision on the coat, then to the lower level to try different shades of lipstick.

When they got home, Judy stretched out on her bed and stared at the American Girl dolls lined up on the dresser. She knew their names and remembered how each one had felt different to play with. The lipstick was still on her mouth and the taste of it made her wish the dolls would disappear.

That same day, her brother, Michael, went out to Long Island with their father to get basketball shoes at the mall. They were the newest ones from LeBron James and everybody at school was getting them. While his father was paying, Michael made a point of checking that he had the right box, with pictures of LeBron James in action printed on the cardboard. He wanted to study them, figure out the links between the photos: were they all from games where LeBron James scored more than a certain number of points? Were they all photos taken at away games? Shots from rookie season? Assists?

Michael explained all this on the drive back to Brooklyn, his father listening with admiration and fear.

Transitions had always been difficult for Rebecca, and any impending separation from her children usually inspired a rush of closeness. Her parents were Broadway entertainers who for decades had worked six nights and two afternoons a week. Now they were retired and lived in the Hamptons, joyfully hosting their grandchildren when she and David had to travel.

It was Rebecca and David's fifteenth wedding anniversary, and they were going to Los Angeles for three days to celebrate. Their son and teenage daughter had never been to Los Angeles but had seen pictures of the hotel where their father proposed. Michael wasn't interested; said it looked too girly, with all the palm trees and pink everything.

Rebecca's parents had talked about going to Hollywood when she was a girl, but never left the West Village, even for a summer. Now they were in Southampton, near the movie theater, with its frame of blinking lightbulbs and old-fashioned black letters. When they got *very* old, their plan was to buy into an assisted-living home for retired actors in New Jersey and live out their last days around the piano, with people who knew the same songs they did.

"You have to understand," they once told Rebecca. "There'll be a time when we can't even take showers, let alone cook or make the bed."

When Rebecca and David traveled, their children had to share a room at their grandparents' house. That was the part Judy used to hate, but now she didn't mind. Her mother said it was because she was growing up. But the truth was she could sleep with her phone on the pillow.

——

ON THEIR WAY home from the sushi restaurant, Judy almost got hit by a car. Traffic was coming fast along Driggs Avenue heading for the Williamsburg Bridge, and Judy was watching a picture of herself upload with excruciating slowness. Michael felt the pull as Rebecca lunged for her daughter's arm, but the car missed by several yards.

"Jesus!" her mother said. "What are you doing?"

When it was finally clear to cross and they were safely on the other side of the road, Rebecca turned to her daughter. "How can I trust you to be out by yourself in Southampton if you don't watch where you're going?"

"I'm sorry, Mom," Judy said, feeling for the shape of her phone in a pocket. It was still warm and she imagined all the data scrolling through it, the people looking at her photo on Twitter—*re-Tweeting* it, *faving* it—what boys might see it and want to *follow* her.

"How can I go away with your father if I can't trust you to cross the street?"

"I always look when I'm alone or with Michael, but when I'm with you or Dad I forget."

"That's true, Mom," Michael said. "When she takes me to Vinnie's Pizza, she always looks. Well . . . she's looked five times out of the six we've been allowed to go there this year, but the fourth trip—which is the time she didn't look on the northeastern corner of Bedford Avenue—was when Dad met us halfway because we didn't have any money, which means we weren't out by ourselves technically, because we returned home with Dad who was carrying the pizza—though she didn't look *before* Dad met us, so does that count?"

"It's okay, Michael," his mother said, squeezing her son's hand. "I understand. I get what you're saying."

As they neared the apartment, Rebecca felt a stab of rage. Imagined her daughter's body in the street, limp and bleeding. Wanted to grab the lapels of Judy's new coat and drive home the point. But knew her daughter was at an age where even the smallest humiliation could shred her confidence, and so Rebecca kept quiet.

JUDY WAS FIVE and Michael only a year old when they moved across the East River to Brooklyn. The city had already changed so much. You could live almost anywhere. They had never thought to search outside Manhattan, but then someone told them about Williamsburg: old factories rezoned into new residences with doormen, gyms, and unlimited parking. Now their bedroom looked out on the city where Rebecca had grown up, a place she and David had once agreed *never, ever* to leave.

In the wake of their move, Rebecca had taken four months off work, and David took two. There were no sushi places then, no endless stream of yellow cabs, no high-fashion hair salons or French pastry shops with back gardens—just an expanse of concrete with weeds rising up through jagged lines, and clouds of dust from thumping demolition sites on every block. She remembers the grit-sound of the baby stroller's wheels on broken sidewalks; her children's fingers clasped over a doll or colored block of wood; the shapes of their bodies and how they moved in her arms when trying to flee. They took baths together then, splashing around with the same toys in the shallow water. The ladybug scissors were still under the sink in a cup, and the thought of them resurrected the smell of clean hair and the softness of nails.

They're still young, she thought, waving to the doorman who buzzed them in—*but not in the way they used to be.*

Rebecca's parents were coming in from Southampton to pick up the kids. They would sleep at the apartment, then drive out fresh in the morning with their grandchildren in the backseat. Rebecca and David were booked on an early evening flight to Los Angeles out of Kennedy.

David worked in publishing. He had a row of cacti on his window that the cleaners would carefully dust. The view from his office was of gray stone, lit windows, and smudges of yellow on the street below as taxis queued at red lights. He had been with the same company for two decades. He was known in the book world, and had even worked with a few famous authors. Sometimes writers came in with their literary agents or a private assistant. David preferred his newer discoveries and liked it when they sat in his office in the wake of that first book deal, poring over the contents of his bookshelves.

"These are just a few of the books I've worked on," he would say casually.

In David's mind they were *his* books, but he knew enough about authors not to say it.

Rebecca designed bedding sets for a company based in South Korea and had to take courses at an arts school to keep up with the software. After she decided the pattern and the colors, someone else would prepare the file by filling in codes for the fabric and then making sure the machines did their job. A year later, the sets would be released in home sections of American department stores. Rebecca would take her family to see them, rubbing the fabric and commenting on whether the color was lighter or darker than she had imagined.

ON THE FLIGHT to Los Angeles that night, Rebecca and David caught up on emails, then ordered sandwiches on a touch screen. It had been almost a year since their last trip. A textile conference in Milwaukee where Rebecca gave a speech. David tagged along to see one of his authors read at the Boswell Book Company. They stayed downtown at the Pfister and worked out in the gym together. At night they ordered room service, then made love as the food cooled under silver domes. Cling wrap had been stretched across the tops of the drinks.

When they landed at LAX, a uniformed driver from the hotel was holding a sign. "We should have told him our last name was Godot," David said. "Just for fun."

The driver tried to take their suitcases, but David insisted on wheeling them himself. "The kids will be asleep by now," Rebecca said.

On the 405, David asked if she would ever live a year or two in California. "We could have a pool and a driveway—imagine that."

"You can be the one to tell my parents."

Rebecca imagined herself on the porch at their house in Southampton. "You missed *me* growing up," she would say, "and now you're going to miss your grandchildren growing up as well."

The power of her fantasy surprised and saddened her.

On their last visit to Los Angeles, Rebecca and David stayed at one of the hotel's famous bungalows. Rebecca wondered what it would be like after so long, but David said fifteen years is nothing.

"But for a hotel?" Rebecca said. "Think about it—two people staying for an average of two nights, and one person staying for one night, with, what? Four hundred rooms? The number of guests each week would be, give or take, around—"

"You sound like Michael."

"Well, I am his mother. And I think fifteen years *is* a long time. That's two years longer than Judy's whole life. Think about it, David—more than the whole of our daughter's life since we've been here, yet to us it feels like no time at all."

"That's one way of looking at it," David said. "One of my writers said that life is slow to live, but quick to remember— that's why it feels short, because of the speed of memory. Imagine if it took weeks of thinking to remember a single detail?"

"Weird," Rebecca said.

"Or it just means we're getting old; that's probably what it means."

"We're not *that* old, David. Forty-six is not old, not these days."

David wanted to say more, but knew he would be arguing only for the sake of it. His wife did the same when she was hungry or tired.

After they arrived and were waiting for the porter to bring their luggage, Rebecca and David walked around the bungalow—but couldn't tell if it was exactly the same.

"The bathroom is different," David said. "That's for sure."

Rebecca said the bathtub was new, because the faucets were on the side.

"We can take a bath later, if you're not too tired," he said.

"Funny to think there was someone here last night," said his wife. "Someone in the bed, their clothes on the chair, their things out on the table." David looked at the toilet and imagined an old man with pleats of white skin.

They had ordered a sports car to drive around. It was something they could do only when the kids weren't there. The car had to be delivered to the hotel because the engine was in the back and there was no room under the hood for their luggage.

When they met years ago, David had a green Porsche that belonged to his late father.

AFTER REBECCA PUT her clothes away, she called the restaurant to check they were still serving. "You can have a really good glass of wine," she said, "then after we can stroll back along the brick path." She said she loved California at night. The air was warm, and there was bougainvillea and the aroma of jasmine just pulled you along.

Before dinner, they had a drink. The bartender was in his fifties and had a tight, red face. He shook Rebecca's Shirley Temple as if it were something exotic, then asked where they were in from.

When their table was ready, the bartender put their drinks on a tray. David took a card from his wallet.

"I bet you have a million stories," he said.

The bartender nodded. "You bet."

"Well, if you ever think about doing a book..."

The bartender smiled and took David's card. "Oh, sure," he said.

Then a waitress picked up the tray and they followed her.

Rebecca's heels sounded good on the tile floor and people looked up. She had always wanted a pair of Christian Louboutin shoes, and purchased them the day Judy picked out her new coat.

"Classic," the shoe salesman had said. "And the high platform eases the pitch."

Rebecca blushed when Judy said she liked them too, because in her mind she was wearing them for sex, like the women in the short videos David sometimes watched on his computer before coming to bed.

"To think," David said after ordering another glass of the Caymus cabernet, "It's been fifteen years since I proposed and fourteen since we've been married."

Back then, they both drank. David had purchased the engagement ring a month before from Harrods during the London Book Fair. All Rebecca could remember was the scent of jasmine and the way it seemed to lift her with each breath. In the morning she kept twirling the ring, wondering how it would feel to wear for the rest of her life.

WHEN THE FIRST courses arrived, the waiter saw they wanted to share and brought extra plates.

"The goat cheese is good," David said. "But I prefer the lobster bisque at Silver's in Southampton."

"Maybe my parents will take the kids there for lunch."

"Oh my God, the desserts," David said. "I could go there just for the desserts."

They had been in Los Angeles only a few hours and were already having a good time. After the first course, David reached for his wife's hand. He touched the ring, moved it back and forth along her finger.

"Being with you is really wonderful," he said. "Seriously."

Rebecca blushed. "We're in such a good place."

"There's nothing that could come between us at this point," David told her. "I truly believe that."

Rebecca agreed.

David ordered meat for his main course, while Rebecca tried a white fish she had never heard of. When the plates arrived, the waiter left them alone to eat and talk. David was enjoying the wine immensely.

"Is there anything you've ever wanted to know about me?" he said after a long silence. "Any question you've always wanted to ask? Or something you've always wanted to tell me?"

"Same for me," Rebecca said. "Tell me anything you want, or ask me anything. I'm completely open."

"No, I mean it," David said. "I'm really serious. I want to share everything with you."

They had been through many life events. The death of David's mother; the birth of their children; the 9/11 attacks when Judy was only a few months old, and how worried they were about breathing the air. Then the birth of Michael—and the suspicion of Asperger's when he started school. It was about then their careers really took off, and they could finally go places like Paris and Hawaii.

"You're a great husband," Rebecca said.

David laughed. "Tell me what you mean by that. I'm curious. I really want to know."

"Well, you've never been unkind or unfair, or controlling, like so many people."

Although she did not say it, the only time David had been cruel was when his mother was dying and he was with her all the time. Then he had said things she would never forget—that he was tired of being needed by everyone and dreamed of a different life far away by himself. Rebecca had listened, a lump forming in her throat. Tried to hold him but he didn't want to be held. Didn't want to be touched.

When they had first met, on the uptown N train, David was at a time in his life when he wasn't speaking to his mother at all. Hadn't spoken to her for about three years after dropping out of Amherst College to live in New York City and become a writer.

Then, a few years later, when David proposed in Los Angeles at the fancy hotel, Rebecca insisted he tell his mother the news, try to forgive her, perhaps rebuild their relationship. She said that the way a man treats his mother is an indication of how he'll treat his wife.

David agreed to do it and got back in touch—but it sapped a lot from their own relationship, and was something Rebecca regretted making him do.

When they were on speaking terms again, David's mother bought a studio on the Upper East Side. Sometimes, she would call thirty times in a single day, or in the middle of the night crying—asking David to come over because of a noise, or a pain in her chest, or something terrible she'd seen on the news and thought was happening to her.

Looking after her used the same energy he needed for the relationship. Rebecca coped with it all by drinking, the way she drank back in high school when she was alone or when she felt she was alone.

Not long after they were married, something happened.

It was when David's mother was at her worst, and—although they didn't know it—was in the last few weeks of her life. David was staying at her studio several nights a week and Rebecca was drinking more than ever, going out to bars, having fun with people she never saw again.

When she confessed what had happened, David kept saying, "In our bed? In our bed, Rebecca?"

Then he disappeared. Just vanished, for three whole days and nights.

It was the only time Rebecca felt like killing herself. She had never told anyone but now understood how people were able to do it when she noticed flowers and laminated photographs on the Williamsburg Bridge.

On the fourth day, David came back. Rebecca had cleared out every bottle in the house and left leaflets on the table from a support group for alcoholics.

"THERE IS SOMETHING," Rebecca said, once the waiter had taken their order for dessert. "Something I've always been curious about."

David wiped his mouth. "That's exactly what I mean."

And so Rebecca asked where he was for those three days. It was the only thing she didn't know. The only question she had left.

David stared at her for so long she began to feel uncomfortable seated there in expensive wedge heels and the Italian dress purchased a year earlier for the National Book Awards dinner.

"I thought you'd forgotten about that," he said finally. "Seems like such a long time ago."

"You said *anything*, David—and that's the only thing."

David put down his glass and Rebecca realized he was more than a little drunk.

"I only ask because I feel so close to you," she said, touching his hand. "Because there's nothing that could come between us now."

"That was a tough time."

"What I did, I can never forgive myself for. You know that, right?"

David picked up his glass again, rolled his fingers on the stem. "Well, it's not the worst thing that ever happened in the world."

"It was to me," she said. "Almost losing you, I mean."

"Listen, Rebecca, some people see their families tortured, or lose their kids, or watch them get raped or blown to bits. What happened to us is really not that bad when you look at history."

Rebecca held the napkin to her face. "I'm going to ruin my makeup."

The waiter saw what was happening and took their desserts on a loop.

"I just can't believe you came back," she said. "I always wondered what made you come back."

She had imagined a lover, an old flame from Amherst who wore black glasses and men's shirts—or some five-star hotel on the Upper East Side, where girls discreetly work the bars and the restaurants.

"I was worried you were dead."

David laughed, "It almost happened. After staying with a colleague in Westchester for two days, my plan was to drive north to Montreal to clear my head. I'd always thought I could live there, in Canada, and if anything ever happened, it was a place I knew I could go start over. But then on the journey north it started raining so bad, I couldn't even see out the window, and the fan in that old Porsche didn't work, so I was struggling just to stay on the highway—just to see where I was going."

"I loved that car," Rebecca said.

"It was my father's, did I ever tell you that?"

Rebecca said she knew.

"Well, anyway, with the rain and the blower not working, I had to turn off and find a motel."

"What happened then? What did you do there?"

"I found myself a few miles outside a little town in upstate New York."

"What was the name? Have we been there?"

"I can't remember," David said. "I could probably look it up, but I couldn't tell you now."

IT COULD HAVE been anywhere and wouldn't have mattered. After checking into a roadside motel, David took a long shower. Then he sat on the bed drinking black coffee and listening to the rain. His wife had cheated on him and he had to decide if he wanted a divorce and where he was going to live and what he was going to do with his mother, who needed full-time care.

He reached for the television remote on his side table, but the sound of people laughing and going about their lives made him panic, so he pulled on his corduroys, buttoned up his shirt, and went back outside. At first the car wouldn't start, so he let it sit, figuring he'd flooded the engine by pulling too hard on the choke. It had stopped raining by then, so he walked to a gas station and bought cigarettes. A girl he wanted to have sex with in college used to smoke Merit Lights in his room listening to Nick Drake. She wore long cashmere sweaters over bare legs. When he felt himself getting hard, he marveled at the unsentimental logic of his body and imagined his wife at home in their apartment, lights off, motionless on the bed, makeup all smudged like marks from a fire. He couldn't decide if her eyes were open or if they were closed.

It was still too early to feel anything except fear.

Would she be someone he would come to hate? Or pity? Someone for whom he would feel nothing?

The man in the gas station told him town was five miles up Route 17, and there were places to have dinner on Main Street, burgers and such.

The rain had stopped but the road was still very dark and David had to lean forward in the low seat to see. When he got near town, he parked and walked toward the lights of Main Street. He wasn't hungry anymore, but it felt good to move his legs. He tried to imagine when in history the brick buildings had appeared grand, with candles or oil lamps glowing in all the windows. Now most stood empty, on the verge of collapse, riddled with rats and mold. He wished he were back at the hotel in the shower where it was bright, and he could stand there and close his eyes under the steady water.

But just before turning around, he noticed lights moving up ahead on the sidewalk, and wondered whether it was a shop open late or some local bar.

When he got there, the windows were fogged so he put his

face right up to the glass. Inside, an audience of about thirty or forty people was seated in perfect stillness as children clambered about on a makeshift stage. David could see their bodies darting to and fro in costumes made from old curtains and bedsheets, could hear their heavy shoes dragging over the hollow wood, up and down the stage steps.

The street was still completely deserted, and no one inside seemed to notice he was there.

In the wings, someone was operating spotlights by hand. These were the lights that had beckoned him. He couldn't tell what play it was, but could hear the voices of the children and make out their cries. Things they had rehearsed again and again were finally happening for real.

Then a child climbed onto the stage by herself and started to sing. When David strained to see, he could tell from her face that the girl had Down syndrome.

The other children, still in their costumes, had gathered at either side of the stage. Taller ones at the front knelt down as though in worship.

When the girl forgot the words halfway through the song, her tongue went quickly in and out of her mouth, and she turned her body from side to side as the piano went on playing. David could not see into the room well enough to tell if she was embarrassed, but knew that she was, could feel it in his body as he stood there, and knew that others could feel it too. It was the biggest night of the girl's life. Nothing like this had ever happened to her before. She had been so nervous about messing up it was hard to breathe.

Then a heavyset man in the audience reached quickly for

the hand of the woman next to him, and it was suddenly clear to David that the girl standing alone on the stage was actually his wife, but also his mother—even the man Rebecca had taken into their bed a few days before. And he felt sorry for them, and for himself, and was no longer afraid.

Private Life of a
Famous Chinese Film Director

LONGWEI KISSED HIS sleeping wife goodbye. Her body lay under a single sheet, sculpted by dawn into a shape he would use one day in a film to convey unavoidable longing.

It was very early and the studio car waited outside in the Chaoyang district of Beijing. The driver was tough-looking and wore a gold link bracelet that seemed too loose to stay on.

There was little traffic, and the city was soon far behind in a cloud of yellow-and-gray smoke. The driver's clear flask of tea tilted as the car pulled around corners. Longwei did not speak to the driver, but tried to imagine his life from the details that stood out to him.

The flight to Zurich landed early. It was a short runway, so the pilot had to slow the aircraft quickly. Longwei had slept for a few hours and dreamed he was a boy on vacation with his family in Hangzhou. In the dream, lake fishermen drifted home through evening currents, steering their narrow boats under footbridges. The water was soft and bright. There were real memories sewn into the fabric of the dream: Longwei's father walking ahead on his own, then turning to look at them all from a distance, as though he were a ghost remembering happiness.

They lived then in a hutong alley community, where his father sold vegetables on a corner.

After a short flight to Mallorca from Switzerland, Longwei was met by the senior manager of a private villa where he planned to finish his latest screenplay, *Tai Chi Flaming Fist*. It was the sequel to his last film, *Shao Lin Pirate Monks: Revenge of the Grasshopper*.

The manager spoke several languages, but Mandarin was not one of them. Longwei noticed his expensive shirt, strong hands, and other details that suggested the man had once been a soldier.

Once outside the city of Palma, the two-lane road gradually narrowed to a dark strip that wound through the mountains. Villages had been whittled into the rock above, and stone houses dotted hillsides of wild, rough grasses.

Longwei considered Europe a living museum as it had come to terms with its past. His wife loved Paris and they often travelled there together—though after a while, Longwei would miss coffee-flavored tea, red bean buns, and the colorful sweep of ballroomers in Tiantan park. He hadn't considered Mallorca, until one of the studio heads in Beijing told him about a luxurious villa outside the village of Deia, perfect for writing and solitude.

Over the next few days, Longwei ate in the kitchen with the house-chef and read international newspapers. He swam in the pool, then lay in the shade listening to birds, watching them drop in arcs from tall trees and fly out over the water.

He switched off the air-conditioning in his room, and slept on top of his covers with the windows open.

For almost a week, Longwei did not look at his script, nor

make any notes on the story. The staff at the house found him easy to please but couldn't tell if he was happy. He called his wife at strange hours, and was surprised by late-night burlesque scenes on the German or Dutch television channels.

He had met his wife in Ningbo at a crowded railway station. They were both sixteen. She worked in a factory and her mother and father worked there too, though at mealtimes she would sit with her friends.

One afternoon, while Longwei was exploring the gardens of the villa, he took a steep hillside path down to the bay.

There were many sheep, and they stopped eating to watch him pass. In some tall, dry grasses, he noticed a young lamb. Its mother was licking the wet skin. The lamb had no fur and its legs were shaking. Longwei wandered if eating meat would be considered barbaric by future generations.

There was no one around when he reached the sea. It was rocky but the water was calm. He took off all his clothes and swam naked for the first time since he was a boy. His body looked small and white, and made Longwei think of the pearl earrings his wife kept in a blue velvet case. He wondered if there were fish swimming near that he couldn't see, or if a current would carry him into deeper water. He pictured his wife on the rocks wearing sunglasses, then heard her voice telling him to come in.

AFTER A WEEK at the villa, the manager showed Longwei the location of two ancient stone lookouts called miradors. He explained that people had once stood guard there, keeping watch for invading fleets. The next day, Longwei visited them on his own. Each mirador was so high on the cliffs, and the wind so strong and incessant, that the silence descending seemed holy, as though one could be cleansed by a violent experience of solitude.

There must have been periods, Longwei told the house-chef over dinner, when for whole generations nothing at all happened, and so the act of keeping watch would have become a sort of ritual meditation.

He imagined how the Mallorcan villagers must have taken turns in these ancient stone parapets, from which hundreds of miles of open water could be swallowed in a single glance. Many would have fallen asleep, especially on windless, star-filled nights.

The chef was interested in what Longwei was saying, and wondered how the stars must have looked before electric light came to the island.

When he cut the fruit for dessert, Longwei described the small mountains of bitter melon, celery, bok choy, and cabbage that used to fill the back of his father's Shanghai Forever tricycle.

At the end of almost two weeks at the villa, Longwei decided to write something new and leave his unfinished screenplay in the Goyard duffel his wife bought him in Cannes as a late birthday present. The pattern on the bag reminded Longwei of Islamic architecture: the intricate, deliberate repetition without beginning or end, an intelligence beyond human understanding.

Shooting for *Tai Chi Flaming Fist* was scheduled to begin late autumn in Ningbo, then wrap up in Beijing two months later.

It was a huge budget, and the studio wanted casting decisions as soon as possible, with big stars in the lead roles, and of course Longwei's usual grand fight scenes to ensure success in the provinces and overseas market.

After almost three weeks in Mallorca, Longwei called his wife in the middle of the night to ask about the weather in Beijing. She felt sorry for her husband, because he was far away and needed her in a way he couldn't admit. But she had been married to him a long time, and knew that loneliness was part of his creative process.

Longwei eventually confessed to her that *Tai Chi Flaming Fist* was no longer the film he wanted to make; even the sight of the script on his desk at the villa, filled him with despair and boredom. His wife worried what the studio would say, but Longwei reassured her that it was the beginning of a new way for him as an artist, and that his old films seemed somehow thin to him now and relied too heavily on things he knew people would pay to see, but which had no deeper significance.

Longwei told his wife that the next picture he made would be a sort of comedy, based on the people he had known growing up in the hutong community in Beijing. The action would not come from fist or foot—but from memory, and the struggle to keep a hold of our lives.

His wife asked if it would be a love story, reminding Longwei how they found each other as teenagers at the railway station. She asked if he remembered the night markets, and they laughed about sharing single bags of Ningbo fried batter, so their hands might accidentally touch.

It was almost five A.M. when they finished talking. The

garden outside Longwei's room was coming back as night drained. He lay there going over their honeymoon in Hokkaido. The tops of mountains like white fists.

His new film would be like his very first film. The one he made with a handheld camera at the Ningbo night market as a teenager. He would sit down and let the story write itself from start to finish, then send in the script without telling the studio what it meant. There would be an uproar, he knew that: people screaming, bottles of Johnnie Walker Blue Label hurled as men and women lost face with studio heads.

But in time they would see he was right. They would catch up.

There would, of course, be new conditions with a picture like this. The studio might want him to finance a portion personally, until audiences could get used to the new genre.

But Longwei believed so strongly in his vision, that with his wife's blessing—he was prepared to finance the entire picture himself. This would almost certainly give him final say on the last scene, because, although he was yet to write the script, he knew instinctively, there could be no people in the shot:

Just a tiny hutong home,
with an old spring bed,
a vase of blue flowers,
full moon drifting. . . .

WORKING SCRIPT/STORY NOTES

Beijing/Ningbo Shooting Crew

Golden Helper II

An Epic Fable of
Wealth, Loneliness, and Cycling

A New Film
by
PENG LONGWEI

Chinese Translation by Li Chen of Bethel, China
Home for Blind and Visually Impaired Orphans

Inspired in part by the true story

Restoring the Light

A documentary film by Carol Liu

意识是改变的第一步。

...awareness is the first step for change...

—

For a long time,
Golden Helper II was just a lump of metal welded
to the frame of a crooked tricycle
used to ferry small mountains of bok choy
(and occasionally celery)
to a street corner in Beijing opposite Chanel
where blind Mr. Fun and his wife
had their vegetable business.

The idea for Golden Helper II had appeared in Mr. Fun's head
one night at the kitchen table
searching for a home in the world like fire or the wheel.
Mr. Fun folded pieces of newspaper to help him remember—
couldn't draw his ideas for the same reason he sold vegetables
and didn't work as an engineer,
which was his dream.

Mr. Fun put the pieces of folded newspaper away
in a drawer that wouldn't close because of New Year's cards,
coins, a set of teeth, old keys, plastic toys, souvenirs,
and a whistle;
Mr. Fun's life in small pieces.
Most of his inventions never became anything
more than a folded newspaper,
but he felt Golden Helper II was special,
and Mr. Fun knew exactly where this bundle
of copper, steel, and rippling chains could be welded
onto the frame of the Fun family tricycle.
Mr. Fun's ideas often came in the evening
when Mrs. Fun and Little Weng were at home
watching television, bellies full, eyes closing.
At night he sometimes stood over their beds,
sometimes stood there in the darkness,
his heart like a kite on currents of breath.
It would be like when they were dead, he thought,
except he would be dead too.

No more Fun.

Mr. Fun was also a worrier,
but if there was nothing to worry about,
he let himself be swept up in flights of fancy.
Once he wondered what it would be like to go backward.
He caught the idea from television:
Mrs. Fun staying up to watch Brad Pitt
in the old days of America.
In the movie, the voice of Brad Pitt got younger and younger
until he could only cry, and not say to those around him,
"I was born an old man who played cards, smoking."
When the house was quiet, Mr. Fun imagined living every day
of his own life again in reverse.

... sitting around as Little Weng gets younger and shorter,
until he stops walking, becomes very small,
disappears back into his mother.
He would get younger too, until an eager, sprightly Mr. Fun,
sat listening to a pretty girl (Mrs. Fun) wash clothes
in a bucket for the first and last time.
Little Weng would be lost first, though,
dead without having to die.
What a good thing, he told Mrs. Fun in bed,
that the street of life is one-way.

One of his customers once told Mr. Fun
about a household machine
that could press thoughts into waves of dots,
then be read and understood by anyone
willing to learn this new language.
Mr. Fun described it to his family one night eating dinner.
"There is a machine for everything nowadays," Mrs. Fun said.
Little Weng stood up from the table,
"One day I will be rich enough to buy Dad this machine
so he can learn the language of dots."
"But you are already the richest person in China,"
said Mrs. Fun wisely.
"I mean with money," Weng said. "I'm going to be the first
person in our family to attend university. Then after years of
hard work, will provide a life of comfort for you and dad—
no more bok choy, no more celery—
farewell, bitter melon."
"That's such good news," his mother said.
"But first step: finish noodles."

One night Little Weng couldn't sleep.

And a light in the kitchen meant his father was awake too.

Peeking around the door, Weng saw tomorrow's vegetables

all over the table.

Then he heard his father's voice.

"Think how many rainfalls made each one grow."

Weng went barefoot into the

kitchen, climbed into his father's lap. "Sixteen?" he said.

"Hard to say," replied his father, lifting a tomato to his son's ear,

"but everything inside has entered from the roots."

The windows were violet when blind Mr. Fun

carried his son back to bed.

Day was in night's arms.

The following afternoon when Weng was in school,
his mother had a fright while making his bed.
Mr. Fun was oiling the family tricycle in the kitchen.
It would soon be time for Mr. Fun and his wife
to pick up the afternoon vegetables
and pedal them back to the corner for selling.
"You need to speak to our son," Mrs. Fun said,
standing in the doorway.
"He's been sneaking food into his room."
"Sneaking food?"
Mrs. Fun found her husband's hands.
"What is this?" he said. "A tomato?"
"It was under his pillow!"

Over dinner that night Mrs. Fun saw the funny side.
When she stood to get second helpings, Mr. Fun reached
for her arm and held on. "Mrs. Fun," he said,
"Most of the work in this family falls on you because I am blind,
without you all would be lost . . . you are our golden helper."
Mrs. Fun blushed and went to the stove.
"But you don't know what golden means!"
The words floated around Little Weng's head
as he fell asleep that night.
Moments like this between parents
give children the courage they will need to watch them die.

That was the evening Mr. Fun remembered his latest invention.
And when everyone was in bed, he went to the drawer
(that wouldn't close)
and found the pieces of newspaper
he had folded in a special way
so the idea would not escape.
As a worrier, he knew that life would be hard
for his wife and son
if he happened to die one night on the old spring bed;
Mrs. Fun was captain of the Fun family ship,
But he was the anchor.
That's why he knew this latest invention had to be made,
and how it came to be called Golden Helper II.

He instinctively knew the different parts
and how they should piece together.
Golden Helper II would also be a family of three,
but in metal, with oil for blood.
Over the next several months, Mrs. Fun procured
the different pieces her husband would need to assemble the
mechanism for real.
Some parts were not the right size
and had to be cut again by angry men in the metal shop.
Some pieces were too heavy,
others too light.
Part of the mainspring had to be wound from different metals
to account for summer heat and winter cold.
Mr. Fun could not have asked for a better wife.

When it was finally built, they took turns
holding Golden Helper II in their hands.
"Heavy," Mrs. Fun said. "But I still don't get what it does."
Then she helped her husband put on welding gloves
that reached up to his elbow.
"Think of it like this," Mr. Fun said. "Imagine that, when you
give me a kiss, I take that kiss and turn it into something else,
like a compliment for our son, who turns it into a good deed at
school, and so on and so on, and the energy keeps going, keeps
turning through the universe on the same course, forever and
with no one name."

Little Weng's job was to make sure Mr. Fun didn't catch fire.
The water in his bucket was heavy.
He remembered his father telling him about the sea,
and how it undresses the earth every night.
The welding torch made Mrs. Fun think of New Year.
The dazzle and scent of solder hypnotized her.
How blind Mr. Fun scorched Golden Helper II onto the frame
of the family tricycle is—to this day—a complete miracle.

When it was finished, Mr. Fun stood back
while his family stared
at the smoking, blackened, cabbage-shaped bundle,
bulging with oily strips of metal.
"I have a good feeling about your new invention," said Mrs. Fun.
Her husband thanked her. "Let's hope it works."
Once Golden Helper II had cooled,
Mr. Fun began gathering the other parts,
including three chains, which over the next few evenings
he would thread with painful slowness
through openings in Golden Helper II.

With a few minor adjustments
Golden Helper II *did* work.
Imagine freezing Weng on the backseat of the tricycle,
teeth rattling—small hands pressed into the bun
of his father's belly
who hardly had to pedal on account
of Golden Helper II's magic touch.
Then tiny Mrs. Fun at the front on a horse cushion,
steering around holes in the road, shouting at pedestrians.

二

By the time their son turned sixteen,
nothing seemed like it would ever change,
which usually means it's about to.
One morning Mrs. Fun put on a Sunday dress and a silk scarf
because she had to go out.
Mr. Fun gave her money to pay their neighbor Hui
who sometimes drove them places,
but Mrs. Fun saved it and took the bus.
When she got to the hospital, she told the doctor
she had been uncomfortable for some time.
The pain had been coming and going,
as though it couldn't make up its mind.
She got back late with the smell of chemicals on her.
When she saw her husband and son
at the kitchen table with no bowls
Mrs. Fun started to cry and rushed to the sink,
but her husband stood and said firmly,
"Put down that wok!"

A few days later she went back for the results.
Other people were waiting noisily outside the room,
but the doctor gave Mrs. Fun time to digest the news.
As she waited for the bus home her bag got heavy
and she fell headfirst into the street.
Road sweepers dropped their brushes,
then helped get her a seat when the bus came.
On the journey home Mrs. Fun realized it was time for action
and started making a long list to record for her husband
on the family cassette player.
She imagined the sounds of her voice in the machine,
years after the real one had gone silent.

Here are some of the things on Mrs. Fun's list:

当我们的儿子表现不好的时候，和他开个玩笑，这样他在
承认错误的时候就不会不好意思。

虽然小翁长大了，还是要每天给他一个拥抱。

一定要让他吃，直到他打嗝。

直到他打嗝。直都在看着他，除非他想独处的时候。

独处的时候。谢谢你在天坛公园邀请我做你的新娘。

你送我的那些蓝色的花，这些年来我都把它们养
的很好。

When our son acts badly, make a joke so he's not
embarrassed to admit he was wrong.

Although Little Weng is big now, put your arms
around him once a day.

Make him eat until bursting.

Reassure him I am watching (except
when he wants to be alone).

And thank you, Mr. Fun, for asking me to be your bride
in Tiantan Park. The blue flowers you gave me
I have kept alive all these years.

One evening,
Mrs. Fun asked her husband and son
to lie with her on the old spring bed.
When they woke the next day she was gone.
It rained then. But after that it was clear and bright
with a half-moon drifting.

三

Mr. Fun got old very quickly.
His hair went gray.
He didn't laugh into his soup anymore.
His son had to remind him,
wash your face, Dad, comb your hair.
He never stayed up late,
nor made another model out of newspaper.
Anything that broke he left broken.
Little Weng stopped thinking about university
because his father could not sell vegetables without assistance.
They measured time through old rituals and new ones
forced upon them by absence.

Twelve years passed like this.

It eventually became easier for Weng to leave his father home
where he could keep warm and listen to the television.
But Mr. Fun was soon bored
and wanted to go out in the evenings.
Weng trailed him through the hutong district at twilight,
through the sizzle of woks and the calling out;
past grocers packing their vans,
and the song of bells as parents pedaled home to their children.
He kept a close eye as Mr. Fun stopped every now and then
to turn around and look.
He once told his son:
"The greatest treasure of our lives cannot be seen,
or held, or touched."

Sometimes Weng took his father to hear karaoke
in Tiantan Park.
There was a singer Weng liked who always put his hand
on Mr. Fun's shoulder at the end of a song,
as though the words had been written with *his* story in mind.
The attention made his father eat more
and comb his hair on Sunday
the way he did when Mrs. Fun was alive.
The singer encouraged people to clap along too,
so that Mr. Fun could hear there were others.

Sometimes, when they got home in the afternoon,
Mr. Fun would sit with Mrs. Fun's scarves.
She had kept them in a basket under the old spring bed.
He held each one to his face.
The scarves were silk and many colors.
Each birthday he used to buy Mrs. Fun a new one.
When times were hard, Mrs. Fun went to the shop
a few days before her birthday with one of her old scarves.
She told the woman to look out for the blind man
that was her husband, then said:
"Please sell this old one to him for the price of the wrapping."
Whenever Mr. Fun checked in the basket
under the old spring bed,
he believed his wife kept losing them.
That Mrs. Fun, he thought.

One evening he wandered on to Wangfujing Road
and was almost killed.
When Weng caught up with him, people shouted:
"Get the old man home!"
The next afternoon, the woman who supplied the Fun family
with vegetables advised Weng to tie a piece of rope
to his father's legs so he could go only so far.
Weng thought about it all that afternoon while bagging pea
sprouts
then went home and kicked the leg of the kitchen table
with his worn-out shoe and the leg snapped.
Soup bowls went crashing.
Mr. Fun got up quickly from the old spring bed.
Was it burglars? he thought.
"It's okay, Father," Weng said. "I'm not hurt."
The bowls Mrs. Fun had filled with soup for so many years
lay in pieces.
But Mr. Fun remembered her voice on the cassette,
heard her speak to him.
"If your mother could see us, Weng," he said,
"what do you think she would say?"
Weng swept the floor with his eyes.
"She would say," his father went on,
"'Even though all my bowls are broken,
you can still have another helping.'"

Weng led his father back to the old spring bed,
then took off the old man's slippers and rubbed his feet.
Night was settling around them.
On the blanket Mickey Mouse and Donald were still waving,
after all these years their smiles unbroken.
That's the spirit, Mrs. Fun would have said.

Weng talked it over with his neighbor,
and it was agreed that when Hui wasn't home to keep an eye,
Mr. Fun would go to work with his son.
And there was still the extra seat on the back of the tricycle.
Mr. Fun now held on to his son
the way Weng once held on to him.
And pedaling was easy on account of Golden Helper II,
still tickling away under the frame.
A few strokes took them miles.
Occasionally someone would pass, see them not pedaling
and look down at the metal cabbage welded into the bike
with three chains pouring through.

Weng and his father lived in the old part of Beijing,
where blind Mr. Fun had grown up.
But the hutong districts were disappearing
under shadows of rising concrete and glass.
As the years went by, Weng knew that, one day in the future,
someone would sit staring at a flat-screen television
on a white leather couch
where there had once been a basket of scarves
under an old spring bed,
and a hot kitchen with a drawer that wouldn't close,
and things hung to dry in the windows,
and a sagging, rosewood chair with a red cushion
where blind Mr. Fun used to sit,
listening to his favorite show,
Empty Mirror.

Then, one day,
as Mr. Fun's dinner was being thrown around a wok by his son,
the television went quiet
and he heard a voice he knew.

Felt a hand touch his.

That's exactly how it happened
in the kitchen one night.

Full moon.

四

By the time Weng got used to living without his father,
things in Beijing had really changed. Each day brought at
least one group of tourists into the district.
And Beijing roads had become slow rivers of metal,
a toxic cloud you could see from space.
Weng's community was now penned in on all sides
by shopping centers that sold driving shoes from Italy
and jewels too heavy to wear.
Sometimes Weng stared into the windows of Chanel
still visible from the corner where he sold vegetables.
The dummies behind the glass were dressed for a beach party,
or skiing, or some other activity impossible in Beijing.
His father had once told him:
beauty cannot be bought, only perceived.
Peering at the Chanel mannequins became a ritual that
Weng (like many unmarried men who passed that corner)
quietly relished.

Sometimes, Weng imagined the girls in Chanel coming to life. This is what would happen in eight lucky steps:

1. Weng would like one girl in particular.
2. She would like him too and smile.
3. Then somehow be able to move her legs.
4. He would tap on the glass: *Did you eat yet?*
5. He would invite her to join him at Han Palace.
6. She would confess that she has no money, but loves to sell vegetables.
7. Six months go by.
8. Traditional Chinese wedding.

The owner of Han Palace (Fang) made food extra spicy.
Some of the hot peppers were little balls
with slits like tiny heads laughing.
Fang sometimes sat with Weng as an excuse to drink *baijiu*,
which his wife didn't like because it made him
spontaneously generous with customers.
When it was cold, Weng's neighbor Hui
would bring over containers of noodles,
then sit in the chair with the red cushion and watch Weng eat.
Despite Beijing's ascension in metal and glass,
and the influx of tourists, not much had changed
for people in the hutong.
A new season of grandmothers had begun,
Steaming food was still sold through open windows;
Cars a nuisance, but there were still places
people went to gamble
and places people went to cry.

Weng's parents had lived through the Cultural Revolution.
Their parents through the massacres of World War II,
then civil war.
So much had taken place in the hutong district
where they lived.
But still, clothes of all sizes hung on frayed lines
between light poles and awnings, from morning until dusk.
In summer, when it was too hot, people would carry small seats,
ma zha, outside. Fan their children to slumber.
Sometimes Weng went out to buy tea or a single cigarette,
or just walk,
or sit quietly on a plastic chair,
reading the newspaper.

Everyone remembered his parents,
but only his neighbor Hui came over regularly.
And each day, Weng took the Shanghai Forever family tricycle
to the corner, came home for lunch, ate with the radio on—
then returned for the afternoon shift.
Whatever remained at dusk,
Weng would cook for his own dinner.
Then watch television.
Laugh out loud to himself washing dishes.
The old spring bed was his now, and in the evening,
in the darkness
when he closed his eyes and cycled through childhood,
felt it was almost certainly true,
the best years of his life were gone.

五

Sunday was Weng's favorite day
and started with a coconut bun and coffee-flavored tea.
Then ironing a white shirt and mouse-gray trousers.
He spat on his black shoes, then, with an old bedsheet,
rubbed until he saw his face balloon in the toes.
He fastened his father's Hong Kong sock garters
just below the knee,
then clipped on a dark blue tie.
It was twenty minutes on foot to Tiantan Park.
Sometimes he bought *tanghulu* on a stick,
turning his head sideways to eat.
Over time Weng had become friends with the singer
who was kind to his father.
Uncle Ping was quite a bit older than Weng,
but they still had a lot to say.
Uncle Ping was one of the best singers in the park,
and had a Weibo account with 6,345 followers.

Sometimes people hired Uncle Ping to sing at their parties,
and he had been on television twice—once for his singing,
and the other by accident.
One afternoon, between karaoke sets, Uncle Ping told Weng
that his niece was ballrooming
at the other end of Tiantan Park.
When they got there, Cherry was on a bench drinking tea
holding a hat with a cartoon squirrel on the side.

Uncle Ping introduced them.

"Weng used to bring his father to hear me sing."

Cherry smiled. "Did he have a favorite?"

"'Blue Flowers,'" Weng said.

Cherry said she'd heard of it. "It's one of the old ones, right?"

"But one of the best," her uncle added. "Quite sentimental."

Weng said it was also his mother's favorite.

Cherry nodded. "Then I understand why it's special."

A few Sundays later, they were all in the park
when Uncle Ping looked at his cell phone
and had to leave quickly.
Weng and Cherry spent the afternoon not saying much
but agreed to meet again.
The following week, however,
they almost walked past each other.
Cherry had changed her hair
and was wearing it in an old-fashioned way,
and Weng was in sunglasses
he'd found in the drawer that wouldn't close.
Cherry's shoes were also new,
but when Weng asked she said,
"These old things?"
After sharing a whole spicy fish at the Golden Chicken
they returned to Tiantan Park to hear karaoke
and admire the ballroomers.

One Sunday Uncle Ping sat with them, sharing out sweets.

"My niece and I were wondering if you would ballroom with us next Sunday?"

Cherry touched Weng's sleeve.

"I think you would be successful if you tried."

Uncle Ping said, "We're not getting any younger."

Then he gave Weng another sweet.

"C'mon," Cherry said. "You may as well try."

But Weng just stared at the sweet in his hand.

"Bashful?" Uncle Ping said. "Nothing wrong with that."

It took two weeks for Uncle Ping and Cherry
to persuade Weng to try ballrooming.
"Some people even dance without partners . . . ,"
Cherry kept saying as she showed him basic steps:
quick-quick, slow, quick-quick, slow . . .
" . . . but the important thing is they're dancing."

Fairly soon, Weng was doing something he had never imagined,
with a large chattering group who descended en masse
to dance and sometimes try out their voices.
It was an unspoken law that the older a person was,
the earlier he or she had to arrive at Tiantan Park.
Apartments that skirted the boundaries
were getting harder to rent,
as karaoke machines were in full swing by first light.
Sometimes Weng and Cherry got to Tiantan early.
Listened to songs they had never heard,
then drank coffee-flavored tea in little bakeries,
watching the steam
roll from boiling pots.
Weng even bought a cell phone so Cherry could send him texts
to encourage his steps,
or just friendly symbols like this:

☺☺☺

For Cherry's thirtieth birthday Weng gave her a silk scarf.
They celebrated in a small restaurant where three roads meet.
When Weng asked if she liked her present
Cherry told him she was married.
"I also have a daughter named Shirley," she said.
All the uneaten dishes of food on the table
made Weng feel foolish.
He put some money down and went outside.
Cherry appeared a few moments later.
"You should have told me before I gave you
one of my mother's scarves," he said.

Cherry fingered the silk knot around her neck.
Her hands were dry and callused from long shifts
in the factory where she worked.
"Where is your husband?" Weng asked. "With Shirley
in your hometown of Ningbo?"
"It's a long story."
"Why don't they live here with you? I don't understand."
"Someday I'll explain the situation," she said.
"But it's shameful, I warn you."
"Why did you come to Beijing alone? Isn't there plenty
of work in Ningbo?"
"Uncle Ping got me a better job here as I also
support my parents."
When it was almost dark they parted at the edge of her district.
"All this time," Weng said, "I thought your
uncle was a matchmaker."
Cherry untied the silk scarf and held it out.
"Keep it," he said. "Even though you're married,
today is still your birthday."

六

For the next month, Weng didn't iron his white shirt
nor his mouse-gray trousers, nor clip on his tie
or the sock garters from Hong Kong.
And each evening, as he packed up his vegetables,
the mannequins of Chanel
were transformed by twilight into a window of Cherrys.
One evening, Uncle Ping came to see him,
said he'd heard from Cherry what happened,
and felt responsible for not telling Weng sooner
about his niece's situation.
They sat very still before cooling cups of tea.
Weng turned off the television to be polite.
At last Uncle Ping spoke. "Did Cherry tell you
that I was once almost married?"
Weng shook his head.
"She was so beautiful I couldn't look at her."

"It was hard in China then, with Mao and the Red Guards,
your parents probably told you. But after a few months of
dating, the thought of marriage pulled on us
like a fish to be reeled in.
Back then, if she was to leave her parent's house,
we had to be married.

"We were thinking of some nice hall. A lucky day.
Everyone in red.
But then, one morning, my beloved failed
to show up at our usual time.
I went to her house. Her mother said she was very ill
and I should call again in no less than a week.
But after three days I stood in the rain below her room,
in case she opened a window, I would at least glance her face.
I was quite romantic then, Weng—not like now,
where my only excitement is from karaoke and Weibo.
When seven days had passed I went back
and we sat at the kitchen table not talking.
It seemed her short illness had changed her,
and over the next few weeks
she would not talk about our wedding plans,
and made excuses not to see me.

"One day I asked if she could tell me,
what month we should have the wedding?
And she said I must go back home and never see her again.
When I asked why, she covered her face.
Anyway, I defied her wish and continued to visit.
Finally I got a letter saying that she wanted to break up.

Talk about angry.

"My parents were bitterly disappointed and I was ashamed.
After one month I went back to her house in the early morning.
Her mother came to the door. Asked calmly what I wanted.
Her little sister was standing behind trying to see;
In my frustration I shouted out:

Does your older sister have another she is engaged to?
IS THERE SOMEONE ELSE IN THERE

RIGHT NOW

IN MY SEAT

EATING BUNS?

Her mother closed the door, and I never went back.
In time I just learned to accept my disappointment
like everyone else in the world.

"But that's not the end of my tale," Uncle Ping told him.
"A few months later I woke in the middle of the night,
because there was knocking on my window shutter.
I looked out cautiously, expecting to see something sinister,
but it was my beloved shivering in the darkness.
I rushed around to the front door,
led her inside, heated some water.
I had so many questions but was afraid of scaring her away.
She told me she had been in Shanghai.
Wouldn't say why. *Did she have someone there?* I thought.
A Shanghainese?

"Then she said—and even now I'm a little shy to say it:

Make love to me, Ping

We had only kissed before,
so you can understand I was hesitant.
But I put my teacup down and helped her into my small bed.
She put her arms around me.
It was like a film, but with breathing for music.
When we woke, dawn had come.
She asked if I would take her home and sing.
We held hands and swayed through the alleyways.
She could hardly walk as though seeing me
had made her sick again.
Anyway, I sang a few songs. Kept her hand in mine.
In my naïveté I thought we were back together,
but the next day I went to her mother's house
and found it empty.
A neighbor called to me from a window,
said they had gone in the night.

"For the next few years, anytime she came into my head,
a part of me hurt.
There was no relief. And I never saw her ever again, Weng.
Over the years, other women came and went.
I got on very well in my job, with a reliable income.
But my heart had tightened like a southern fist.
Some girls I met wanted to marry—but I was stubborn,
so they went on to marry others and have nice lives.
In the end, to be happy, it's not enough to love someone,
you also have to accept something in return.

"A few years ago, about when I turned sixty-eight,
I fell down at a restaurant.
The waiters thought *too much grape alcohol,*
but felt guilty later for not rushing over.
At the hospital, the doctors said
there was a problem with my heart
and I would need an operation.
A chance I might not wake up after.
Say your good-byes now, they told me.

"For a long time after surgery I stayed in bed.
At night, when the nurses drifted like swans through the ward,
I began to think about my life as though it were over,
And I, Uncle Ping, a ghost poking about in the past.
I went through each scene.
Drew up the cast of characters who had been part of my story.
Of course, *she* was who I thought of most,
and still so breathtaking—even in memory,
as though my poor heart had been tricked
into believing there was still hope.

"I began to think about what happened all those years ago,
but this time from her point of view.
I considered what life must have been like
living with her mother and sister in that damp house.
I don't think I mentioned that her father
had passed away when she was young.
I began to feel sorry for her, Weng—to forgive her even.
And it was like falling in love again, but without any pain.

"And in that spirit, I decided to go and visit
her old place near where we grew up.
Fifty years had passed. I put on some nice clothes
and combed my hair.
When I arrived, the house was for sale.
There was a light on inside, but when I glanced at my watch,
it was too late to knock.
So I looked instead through a keyhole.
My heart, Weng, was throwing itself against my ribs
as if trying to get into the house.
Then—couldn't help myself!
. . . I lightly rapped on the door.

"The woman who opened the door was not old,
but seemed frail and done-in.
I could tell she was suspicious, but I was wearing nice clothes,
aftershave, and the Rolex Submariner
I bought in the year of the goat,
so she mistook me for someone interested
in buying her house and invites me in,
tells me she's moving away, needs a quick sale.
Once we were in the kitchen, where there was more light,
Guess what?
I couldn't believe it:
Same table, same dishes, same chairs. . . .
Thought I was dreaming.

"This old woman is my beloved's little sister!
I am not proud to admit what I did next,
but realized that in the disguise of a potential buyer,
there was a chance to finally get the truth.
So I asked if she had grown up in the house.
She said *Yes.*
Brothers or sisters?
She paused for a moment,
then nodded, *Older sister.*
She sensed my anxiety. . . .
Would I like some chrysanthemum tea?
It must have been lonely for her there, Weng,
because near the sink: one set of dishes, one bowl,
one pair of chopsticks, one glass, one teacup.
Silence has many forms, eh?
But I gritted my teeth, kept lying,
told her I was from Shanghai.
She didn't say anything, so I asked if she had ever been there.
She said *once,* last year with the company she worked for.
'You never lived there?' I asked. 'You never moved
away from the house?'

"She told me that, for one year, when she was a teenager,
They had lived somewhere else, but not Shanghai.
Then I asked if *older sister* lived nearby.
She considered the question, then pointed to the window,
'Older sister is on a hillside outside the city.'
Instead of anger, Weng—instead of desire, I felt something else,
a sort of lightness, and truly hoped she was with a devoted
husband, children too, even grandchildren,
a house full of voices like a forest in spring.

" . . . Little sister went on talking. *'I don't visit*
as much as I used to, but
at least she is there with our father—
and our mother is out there now too.
I'm the only one left, and so the house that was
once too small is now too big.'
It sounds silly, Weng—but it took me a moment
to realize what she was saying.
'I can see my story has depressed you,' she said finally,
'but the end of my sister's life was happy—because she knew what
love was like, got to taste it before she died with a boy who lived
nearby. Whereas I have lived a whole life and still don't know how
it feels.'
I wanted to speak up! Cry out! Pull the sister toward me!
Tell her: *I was that boy!*
But all I could do was fix my eyes
on some object in that kitchen,
with little or no meaning.

"At last I said, 'What happened to the boy?'

The little sister shrugged. *'She never told him she only had a year*
to live when she broke off the engagement—
wanted to spare him a lifetime of grief.'

'He probably thought she didn't love him,' I said.

'Yes, I've never decided which was worse,' Little Sister answered,
'to lose the person you love after one year?
Or to think they never loved you in the first place?'

For a while neither of us spoke.

Then little sister looked me in the eye.

'Sometimes I think about him and go over in my head
what I would say if we were ever to meet again.'

"I visited that hillside cemetery the next day, Weng.
Then a few days later, I went again.
Then again.
I began practicing the songs she loved
and realized I still had my voice,
though it had been silent for a long time.
When I go there now, other people visiting the graves
of their loved ones mistake me for her husband.
So in the end, Weng, you can see that I got some of my wish."

Then Uncle Ping wrote down the poem that was carved into
his beloved's memorial:

我对你的感情就像最深山谷里的野花,
尽管肆意疯长却无人知晓。

My feelings for you are like the wildflowers
Of the deepest valleys:
Though their abundance increases,
There are none that knows.

七

The following week, Weng was involved
in a serious road accident.
Witnesses saw a man fly off his tricycle into the guardrail.
What bad luck, they all said.
For a few moments after impact, Weng didn't move.
People thought the worst.
But then he opened his eyes and stood quickly,
cursing not out of anger but embarrassment.
The driver of the Rolls-Royce that hit Weng was furious too,
but then an old woman spoke up and waved her cane,
ordered Mr. Yi to help Fun Weng pick up his vegetables.

The smell of onions reminded Mr. Yi of his father's clothes
when he came in from the fields. When the police arrived,
the old woman explained what happened and what she had said
about family and ancestors—how she had used
her cane to restore harmony.
The police looked at the mangled tricycle,
couldn't believe Weng was not injured.
Volunteers carried the twisted frame to the sidewalk as Mr. Yi
noticed a cabbage-shaped bulge of metal welded to the tubing.
"What's that?" he said, pointing.
The volunteers looked too.
"Golden Helper II," Weng said.
"But what is it?"
"It's something that makes it easy to go a long way."
Mr. Yi examined the mechanism more closely.
"But what does it do?"
Everyone on the street was now fascinated
with Golden Helper II.
"It helps with my family business . . . " Weng said. "In a
golden way."

Mr. Yi thought he was being funny.

"Where's Golden Helper I?"

"Dead," Weng said.

"Dead? How?"

"Passed away in bed one night."

The crowd didn't know whether to laugh or cry.

Mr. Yi shook his head. "I'm sorry, but I don't understand you."

"Golden Helper II was named after my mother."

"Your mother's name was Golden Helper I?"

Mr. Yi bent down and touched the mechanism with his hand.

"It's still hot! How does it work? A dynamo? A current through motion? And look! Your tricycle has three chains."

"It was my father's idea," Weng said. "He got it one night after my mother found a tomato in my bed."

Then the policemen got impatient,

thought Weng was a lunatic,

wanted to know where he lived. Traffic was backed up for miles, angry voices crackled from their walkie-talkies.

"Drive this man home!" They barked at Mr. Yi.

But Weng refused to leave without
his vegetables and Golden Helper II.
Could he put them on the backseat of Mr. Yi's big car?
Was there some rope to tie the frame of his tricycle to the roof
of the Rolls-Royce?
In the end, Mr. Yi agreed to buy
all the vegetables for a good price,
and told the crowd of people watching,
Please take free onions and cabbages.
At first they were shy, but after one person
grabbed a bundle, the pile disappeared.
Mr. Yi also pleaded with Fun Weng to let one of his men deliver
the broken tricycle frame to his door as soon as they could get a
truck through the traffic.
The crowd watched as the vegetable seller
was driven away in Mr. Yi's fancy car.
What good luck, they all said.

"Is this a Rolls-Royce?" Weng asked, pushing buttons.

"Don't touch, Mr. Fun, please."

"My father loved cars," said Weng. "He was blind
but would have put his hands on everything—
taken things apart even."

Although Mr. Yi was a solitary person who rarely enjoyed the
company of other people, there was something about the
vegetable seller he liked, and surprised himself by going into
detail about his humble roots in Guanshan village (Hunan
Province), where he was raised on a pig farm.

"My father was *just* like yours," Mr. Yi insisted.

"Always inventing things...."

"Yes," Weng said. "Mine was always doing something."

"Mine too," Mr. Yi said, "Once he even built
a ten-foot-high platform
above the river that flowed near our farm.
Every morning he would launch
pigs off the highest plank into the water
because he thought it boosted appetite."

"Whose appetite?" Weng asked.

"The pigs' of course, Mr. Fun."

Mr. Yi's car inched through the hutong district,
past stands of fruit, small children playing,
people squatting to eat.
Even though Mr. Yi was only forty-nine,
his father was also dead.
Heart attack. Chopsticks on the ground,
and Mr Yi, with all his money,
helpless as a pauper.
Weng thought of both their fathers sitting somewhere together
like the plastic wise men used to decorate bonsai trees.
Weng told Mr. Yi to stop when they were outside his home.
"I'm sorry about the accident, Fun Weng,
but glad you're not hurt.
I'll provide you with a brand-new tricycle within a few days."
"I don't want another," Weng said firmly. "The Shanghai
Forever tricycle was my father's and *must* be returned."
"I'll do my best," Mr. Yi said. "Truly I will."

The next few days were torture,
for Golden Helper II did not come home.
Weng's knee was also hurt. It swelled up and he couldn't walk.
Sitting alone in the kitchen, Weng ate his dinner from cans.
He had also fallen into the habit of checking
his cell phone for text messages,
amazed at how nothing can also bring unhappiness.
Weng remembered the day he bought it
and first showed it to Cherry in the park.
"I got it for a good price," he had said, flipping it open and shut.
"And it's only two years old."

八

After ten days, Fun Weng stared at himself
in the bathroom mirror.
He had lost Cherry and Golden Helper II.
But at least his knee was better.
His neighbor Hui, had an old Pigeon bicycle
in his bedroom with plastic over it.
Weng watched him put on new tires,
then gulp oil across the chain.
"It hasn't been ridden since Mao died," Hui told him.
"But we all have to work, Fun Weng."
The next day Weng transported what produce he could
in large bundles strapped to the frame.
But it was less than half his usual cargo.
Without Golden Helper II, Weng got a taste of what other
cyclists had been going through all these years.
It made him sad to think what his mother
would have said about all his misfortune.
Once, on the old spring bed,
In the middle of the night,
he sat up and said her name.
Over time, he thought, *a person can get used to anything.*

Almost two weeks after the accident, there was a knock at his door.

The driver had been trying to find Weng's address all morning. A few of the neighbors came out to watch as an electric tricycle was lowered off a flatbed truck.

The driver asked Weng to sign some papers.

"It is our best model, Mr. Fun—even before Mr. Yi called in the customization."

"But where is Golden Helper II?" Weng asked. "Where is my old tricycle?"

"What do you want something old for?" the driver said, lighting a Baisha cigarette. "This has a lightweight high-side bed, built-in electric lights, heated seat, heated handgrips, air-horn, radio, CD player, DVD player, low-tire-pressure warning system, GPS, and custom Chanel handlebar gloves."

A sticker on the frame in writing Weng couldn't read said:

Racing Monument Paris
Tour de Farce

But in the days that followed, Weng could not
fully enjoy his new machine.
He went back to where the accident occurred.
Talked to the man in the magazine kiosk,
but learned nothing new.
Contrary to his promise, Mr. Yi had ordered the wreckage of
Fun Weng's tricycle be taken to his apartment
in the central business district of the city,
where he spent several days examining Golden Helper II
in his English pajamas and blue velvet slippers.
It was impossible to dismantle without destroying—
and so Mr. Yi just stared at it, concluding that it was not a
complicated mechanism,
but simply one that hadn't been thought of.

Each evening, Mr. Yi drank single malt
and looked at the broken tricycle in his front room,
marveling at how so basic a principle
could have escaped the engineering minds of history.
When Mr. Yi's friends came over for dinner one night,
they sat admiring the mangled tricycle too.
His business partner's wife liked it so much,
she demanded the name of the gallery.
"I want one for the third guest room," she said.
"Chinese art is so real!"
When the fruit came, Mr Yi told his business partner
that the metal egg mechanism known as Golden Helper II
could potentially be a candidate for mass production.
He explained what he thought it did,
and how it might take a team of skilled engineers
weeks—even months—to reproduce it exactly.
The business partner looked worried,
didn't know where Mr. Yi found it, was afraid to ask.
Was that blood on the frame?
Or sriracha?

That night Mr. Yi was trying to sleep
when a voice woke him.
At first he thought he was dreaming, but then he heard it again.
He sat up in the darkness and blinked a few times,
then noticed a dark figure at the bottom of his bed.
"How did you get in? What do you want?!"
The figure just laughed.
"Please tell me what you want! Take anything!"
"Calm down," the figure said. "I'm not a thief."
Mr. Yi could tell from the voice that it was a woman
and he wondered if one of his staff hadn't let her in
before going home for the night.
"If you are not a thief, then what are you?"
"I'm a ghost," the figure said coming toward him.
Mr. Yi put his head under the covers.
"I don't know which is worse!"
"Well," said the ghost, "that all depends."
"Depends?" said Mr. Yi. "On what?"
"On whether you plan to cheat my son, Fun Weng."

"No. *No!*" Mr. Yi protested. "I'm an honest man—let me explain, Mrs. Fun, *please*, I'm actually trying to *help* your son."

"That may be how you feel, Mr. Yi—but there was a time when you would not have kidnapped a poor man's tricycle because you saw opportunity for yourself."

Mr. Yi said nothing.

"It's not how your parents taught you in Guanshan village."

"Only my mother is alive now," Mr. Yi said.

"But she does not work anymore."

"Why is that, Mr. Yi?"

"Because I send her money."

"And do you know what she does with the money?"

Mr. Yi thought for a moment. "Buys luxury goods for herself? Gets facials?"

The ghost of Mrs. Fun smiled.

"She puts it in the bank, every yuan."

Mr. Yi was surprised.

"In case you ever go broke, Mr. Yi— she can save the day. It's every mother's fantasy."

Mr. Yi was astonished. "But I want her to show off,
have banquets, enjoy a closet of Hermès and Burberry.
Drive any car she wants, or be driven. . . ."
The late Mrs. Fun stared curiously
at the sad figure of the businessman.
"There is a generosity in you," Mrs. Fun said, "but it's
misguided because you're so unhappy with yourself."
Mr. Yi laughed haughtily. "How could I possibly be unhappy?
Look around, Mrs. Fun, look around. . . ."

A few days later, Mr. Yi typed Fun Weng's address
into his GPS system,
but the car didn't seem to understand
anything behind Wanfujing Road.
By noon, Mr. Yi still hadn't found the right hutong district,
and so ducked into a small restaurant called Han Palace.
The owner was watching an NBA game,
but when he saw the Rolls-Royce pull up,
went to get his best *baijiu* and two glasses.

After lunch, Fang (owner of Han Palace) told Mr. Yi that Fun
Weng was a regular, and gave directions to his house.
When Mr. Yi got there, Weng brought him into the kitchen,
then seated him at the kitchen table in the worst chair.
There was dust on the television screen,
and Mr. Yi had to resist the urge to get up
and wipe it with his handkerchief.
Then Weng gave him some tea.
"I had a big lunch with your friend at Han Palace,
and this will break up the grease."
There were photos around the room
of Mr. and Mrs. Fun with their son.
Mr. Yi was drawn to one of them in matching hats.
"Nice picture, that one."
But Weng couldn't wait any longer. "Mr. Yi," he said.
"Where is Golden Helper II?"
"Your days of worrying are over," the businessman said with a
chuckle. "You're going to be one of the richest people in China,
thanks to your father's invention."
Then he leaned in to examine a photograph of Mrs. Fun more
closely. "My only request is that we name it after the honorable
late Mrs. Fun, and drop the II," Mr. Yi said, turning to Weng.
"At least for marketing purposes."

九

Within six months of the accident,
two million Golden Helpers were in use
and the original mechanism had been returned to Fun Weng
in a temperature-controlled glass case,
that was alarmed and bulletproof, with a platinum plaque
that read in diamond script:

GOLDEN HELPER II

(The Original I)

The world was stunned by this miraculous device from China.
International papers hailed Golden Helper
as the first major blow to global warming.

After agreeing on terms with Weng,
Mr. Yi had his factory engineers
work night and day
to configure enormous machines for mass production.
And within weeks, Golden Helpers were being churned out by
the tens of thousands.
In Sweden, entire lanes of highways were designated for people
now able to glide for miles at a time
with only a pump or two upon the pedals—and no emissions.

But even after the first check arrived,
Weng was afraid to stop working,
and every evening after supper
he would take out the check and look at it.
He studied the computer type, the signature, the sky-blue paper
on which it was printed—even the watermark.
The sum was more than his parents had earned
in their entire lifetime,
plus the cost of their home
and probably his neighbor Hui's home too.
He hid the check in Mrs. Fun's scarf box.
It had to be a mistake and he was afraid to take it to the bank
in case there was some law that prohibited
the cashing of enormous checks.
When a second, third, fourth, and fifth check arrived,
each for five or six times the amount of the first one,
Weng wondered if it wasn't some kind of punishment
for not cashing the first one quickly enough,
so he plucked up courage and carried them all to the bank
hidden inside a copy of the *Beijing News*.

When the bank manager heard what was happening,
he rushed out of his office to insist that Fun Weng
have lunch or dinner with him.
But Weng said he had vegetables to sell.
For the next few days after work,
Weng walked the parks near his district,
listening to old songs and wondering
what his parents would have done
with all the money now sitting in the Abacus Bank
like a mountain of gold coins.
Other people would have been exhilarated,
Weng considered one afternoon
as he wrapped the last bundles of bok choy.
A cool wind made him think of the fall songs that would soon
get people ballrooming in Tiantan park.
At least the mannequins in Chanel still excited him,
though not because he imagined one coming to life anymore,
but because there were so many beautiful things
he could now afford to buy Cherry.

And with all Weng's money, she could stop working.
Shirley could have a private tutor.
Their days would be nothing but ballrooming, banquets,
And traveling the world in search of
the rarest Beanie Babies.

A week later, Weng gave the new tricycle away
to a man with a young family
who was just starting out in the vegetable trade.
He also hired a mechanic to fix his neighbor Hui's car,
which had been annoying everyone for months,
billowing smoke into bedrooms.
As the mechanic hammered on the new muffler,
Hui asked Weng why he was being so generous,
and why he had stopped working.
Weng told him that overnight he had become a billionaire
but Hui just walked away, laughing.
After a few weeks, however, people in the neighborhood
began to gossip.

But all Weng could think about was Cherry.
Night after night, he imagined sitting with her
at the kitchen table watching television.
Sometimes on Sunday he woke up very early.
Dressed in the dark.
Then sat on his bed until first light.
But he could not go to Tiantan Park.
Could not imagine dancing alone
like some of the grown men he had seen,
the ones who still lived with their parents
and couldn't make eye contact.

Weng pictured Cherry's husband as a tall and quiet man, holding her hand the way they would ballroom on television with graceful bodies, proud faces.

"His fingers are strong and fine," Weng told himself, "not damaged like mine by decades of vegetable handling... and no scars on his cheeks, either... and of course he speaks well, understands Western manners, doesn't spit... they probably met at work, spent time talking... then many dinners... love declared silently by eyes over crispy duck."

Then wedding day: nice hall (free parking)... the unmarried stare in relief or regret, petals on the ground... a hotel... so charming. Cherry loves the little soaps in the bathroom... rolls them in her hand... her parents will learn to love her new husband as the son they never had. *Big* honeymoon in Hong Kong... no, Thailand (paid for by mother's savings),... *Take photographs*, the mother tells Cherry. *Here's an extra memory card*. Her daughter is happy and looked after. Soon Cherry and her husband have an announcement:

*SHIRLEY
IS HERE*

"She is gifted and generous.
What a family!
It's everything the parents hoped for in a match.
And now a no-good vegetable seller in Beijing
wants to turn everything upside down,
wants to ruin their lives,
tear them apart like a bun. . . ."

In the end,
imagining Cherry's other life was too painful,
so instead Weng remembered how she parted her hair,
And those mornings dancing in the park.
"Don't look at your feet," she would say. "Look at me."

+

One of the agreements Fun Weng
had with Mr. Yi was that the origins of Golden Helper
be kept secret until Weng was ready
to publicly honor his father.
But you may not realize what reporters are like,
how cunning and occasionally evil,
and Weng's hutong district was soon flooded
with men and women asking questions
about giant metal eggs, and tricycles that pedaled themselves.
Weng went to hide out at the Peninsula Hotel
on Goldfish Lane, where he could watch television in the bath.
Mr. Yi began to visit him there,
and they often had morning congee.
After living at the hotel for a month,
Mr. Yi brought representatives
from an American motor corporation to meet Weng.
The hotel prepared a banquet, and everyone
shook hands and bowed.
The Americans were like giants and kept smiling for no reason.
Weng was soon bored by Mr. Yi's talk of money, investment,
and growth, and so after an hour, he excused himself
and rode the escalator
down to the Chanel boutique in the lobby.

Mr. Yi joined Weng for breakfast at the hotel a few days later
because there were contracts to sign.
But Weng instead asked questions like:
Did Mr. Yi have a favorite animal growing up on the pig farm?
What were his best memories of the river?
When did he first know he was allergic to pumpkin?
Does he find snow beautiful or inconvenient?
Then it was Mr. Yi's turn to ask questions,
And one of them led to the story of Cherry.
Oh! To hear her name out loud. . . .

"You really can't control women," Mr. Yi said. "But you shouldn't give up, Uncle Ping sounds clever and probably had a long-term plan. . . ."

"But she has already settled down," Weng told him.

"She has a husband."

"But you say they live apart?"

"Because of work, they live in different cities."

"Sounds suspicious," Mr. Yi said. "Ningbo is a city where there's plenty to do.

I would take a trip down there if I were you,

get a look at this husband."

"Seems like a bad idea," Weng admitted.

"Nevertheless," Mr. Yi said, "you said that Cherry told you it was a long and shameful story, might be worth finding out."

"But I've never been on an airplane, Mr. Yi,

and am afraid to fly."

"Drive, then."

"I don't have a car."

"You can borrow mine. Here's the key—it's outside."

"What if I smash it up?"

"You worry too much, but I'll have the dealer call you."

"I don't have a driving license either."

Mr. Yi laughed. "Does anybody in Beijing?"

At Mr. Yi's request, a Rolls-Royce salesman
picked Weng up the next day,
and they spent most of the afternoon singing in the backseat
to demonstrate the Phantom's great potential for karaoke.
"Would you like a picnic hamper too?" the salesman asked.
"Or a humidor?"
Weng shook his head. "Maybe next time."
"How about I show you the upholstery choices? We have
Moccasin or Oatmeal, with Bird's Eye Maple?
Do you have a time frame in mind for delivery?"
"Next week," Weng said. "I have to go to Ningbo."
"Why don't you fly, Mr. Fun?"
"Because I want to drive. That's the whole reason I'm here."
"Of course, of course," the salesman chuckled. "Driving there is
a luxury few would consider."
"Do you sell driving licenses too?"
The salesman laughed nervously.
"You don't have one, Mr. Fun?"

After a few lessons at Penglun Driving School,
Weng tried his luck on the roads.
The salesman had been calling the driving school daily
to keep track of Weng's progress
and to push for early graduation.
Once in the chaos of Beijing traffic,
Weng tried to remember what the instructor had hold him:
Don't cross into other lanes—but if someone crosses into yours, you
must *fight back.*
In the end, Weng passed his test,
despite rolling over a policeman's foot
outside a school for the disabled.

The first night Weng brought the car home,
Hui came rushing out.
"What's this?" he said. "I didn't know you were a gambler."
"I'm not," Weng said.
"Then how did you get this? You win it in a competition?"
"Yes," Weng said. "That's it."
"Well, be careful," Hui warned him,
"people will look up its value on the Internet."
Then Hui asked if he could sit inside.
"All the celebrities have these," Hui noted,
getting into the driver's seat.
"The keys are in the tray," Weng told him,
"take it for a drive if you want."
"Ha, ha, no," Hui laughed. "A car as valuable
as this should never be driven!"

"I got my license too."

"Wow," Hui said, "all because of a competition."

"But be careful, Fun Weng," Hui went on,

"people are going to wonder why

you're so lucky . . . they're

going to get suspicious."

Weng asked what she should do.

"You want me to be frank?" Hui said.

Weng nodded.

Hui winked, "Spread your good fortune around."

Weng had been assured by Mr. Yi's accountants that
he now possessed a fortune large enough
for a hundred lifetimes.
"Or a hundred people over one lifetime," Weng said.
For his neighbors Weng's unemployment
had become a great mystery they were happy to live with.
Each day was a new good deed: find workers to fix leaky roofs;
hire tutors to help children learn English; put up a wall for old
people to grow flowers against;
the communal hutong bathrooms were now
the only facility in Beijing with heated toilet seats,
deluxe rain showers, steam rooms (with eucalyptus infusers),
part-time attendants, and nightly golf-cart shuttle service.
When people asked how Weng had become so rich,
he told them about his success with competitions.
Soon everyone in his hutong was entering competitions,
and a month later someone won a Jet Ski.

Only Hui was suspicious.

"Know why the oldest tree in Tiantan Park is still there?"

"Because it's ugly," Hui said before Weng could answer.

"Anything that stood out for its beauty or strength was cut
down."

Weng handed Hui some coffee-flavored tea.

They were standing next to each other,

looking at the Rolls-Royce.

"Better come second, even third," Hui winked. "Less attention."

"I only bought it to drive to Ningbo."

"I know," Hui said, going into his house,

"which is why I have a present for you."

A moment later Weng's neighbor reappeared

with a bag of Hello Kitty bobbleheads.

"I got these cheap. Arrange them on the back shelf

of your new car. Then everyone will think you're a joke."

But Cherry was still on his mind.
And though he could no longer see
the logic in driving to Ningbo,
it would at least spare him the sadness
of being in Beijing without her.
The next day, as he was packing for the trip, Mr. Yi came by.
He parked his car next to Weng's, unaware that his neighbors
would now believe Weng had won a second Rolls-Royce.
"I came to see if you're really going," Mr. Yi said.
"You told me it was a good idea."
"Well it probably isn't."
"Why don't you come with me?" Weng asked him.
"Impossible," Mr. Yi said. "It's nothing for you to worry
about—but there are some wrinkles here
that need to be ironed out."
The wrinkles Mr. Yi was referring to
had come about after the release of Baby Golden Helper.
Soon after the first tricycle went on the market, police stations
across China were inundated with calls
from panic-stricken parents
with reports of toddlers filling their pockets
with candy and riding off into the sunset.
One five-year-old-boy was found
three hundred miles from home
trying to buy diapers with chocolate coins.

+—

Weng had never been to Ningbo, but had seen it on the news
when the twenty-two-mile-long Hangzhou Bay Bridge was
first opened to the public.
The news team had been reporting from the middle of the
bridge at a service center called
THE LAND BETWEEN SEA AND SKY.
Weng had also seen a history program on Ningbo,
and he knew there had once been two lakes inside the city,
but only Moon Lake remained,
and Weng imagined people going there at night
to see their faces change in the water.

Weng completed the journey to Ningbo in one very long day,
stopping only for fuel, spicy noodles, and coffee-flavored tea.
At the first gas station, a team of workers swarmed around him.
Weng nodded politely, then went to find the toilet.
An old blind man was outside cleaning his shoes with a tissue.
The old man said he was waiting for his son.
Weng arrived in Ningbo around midnight and checked into
a hotel Mr. Yi had told him about with glass walls
and a dozen different escalators going in opposite directions
with no passengers.

The women at the front desk had gold badges
with their names in English and Chinese.
An older man carried Weng's bag to the room,
then asked if he would inspect it closely.
"It's very nice," Weng said, looking around. "Thank you."
"So, if you had to give it a score,
what do you think would be fair?"
"Very high score," Weng said.
"What about out of a hundred?"
"A hundred out of a hundred," Weng said.
The porter couldn't believe it. "Can I admit to you, Mr. Fun,
that my wife is head of maid services?"
"Then it's the nicest room I've seen in my whole life."
"Please, Mr. Fun, this is too much, you'll bring us bad luck!"
Weng handed the man a stack of yuan,
but in an old-fashioned gesture,
he refused the money and Weng had to stuff
the bills into the porter's pockets.
"Before I go, Mr. Fun, I'm going to linger outside your door for
a few minutes in case there's anything else you can think of that
you might need in the moments following my departure."

In the morning, Weng looked out at the city. He had never been
so high up, and imagined how useful it would be
to have a pair of binoculars.

"Hello, is this Reception?"

"Yes, Mr. Fun, what can we do for you?"

"How do you know my name?"

"I can see it when you call, Mr. Fun, but if it upsets you,
I'll pretend that you're nobody. Do you recognize my voice, sir?"

"Your voice?"

"It's the porter from last night! How does the room look
this morning? Still magnificent?"

"Yes," Weng said, looking at the clothes he had begun to hang
from his suitcase, "I was calling to see if you had any binoculars
or a telescope I could borrow?"

"A wise and original request," the porter said.

They arrived ten minutes later on a silver tray,
and Weng spent the rest of the morning looking out at Ningbo
from the 186th floor.

All those people, he thought,
and not a single one who knows or cares
that I am here or anywhere.

There were two pairs of slippers in a plastic bag next to the bed,
along with body lotion and a shoeshine mitt.
Weng thought of the old man he'd seen cleaning his shoes with
a tissue outside the gas station toilet,
then wondered if his mother and father were together again.
He stayed in his room for the rest of the day and watched
television, though sometimes got up
and went to the window with his binoculars.
At any moment, he thought, *a person is dying or being born.*

He ate in the hotel restaurant that evening,
but the food wasn't spicy enough and the waiters kept coming
over to ask if he'd ever had Champagne.
There were also English translations of dishes
on the menu, such as:
HUSBAND AND WIFE LUNG SLICE, SALIVA CHICKEN,
and ALUMNI PERCH.
When Weng was almost finished with his meal,
a noisy group of foreigners came down on the escalator
and took a table in the far corner,
where they laughed to themselves over bottles of wine and beer.
Weng watched the foreigners eat with knives and forks,
make toasts and cheer one another.
One woman was laughing so much
she had to dry her eyes with the napkin.

After supper, Weng went up the escalator
to a mezzanine level for a foot massage.
He asked the masseuse about her life,
and she spoke about her daughter
and the funny things children say.
When the music stopped, the foot masseuse
left her stool to change the CD.
When the massage was over, Weng unfolded a piece of paper
with the address Mr. Yi's assistant had dug up
for Cherry's family.
"It's not very far from here, Mr. Fun," the masseuse said.
"Do you have a car?"
Weng went back to his room and thought about
what Shirley would look like.
He also thought about calling Uncle Ping, and asking if he
really did have a "long-term plan," as had Mr. Yi suggested.
He also wanted to know if more lucrative work was the only
reason Cherry lived alone in Beijing—
while her daughter, husband, and parents were in Ningbo.
But when he made up his mind to place the call,
he just opened his phone
and scrolled through old messages.

From his window the next morning,
Weng looked down with his binoculars
at children in a schoolyard doing morning exercises.
Like colorful birds, they stretched their wings
to a music no one else could hear.

Weng thought of Shirley again,
wondered if she were one of the colorful birds.
Without binoculars the children were so far away,
but Weng could feel the flutter of their lives
from the 186th floor.
For the next two days he sat in his Rolls-Royce
outside the address he'd been given,
and on the third day he saw Shirley.

He knew it was her because of the blue squirrel hat
he had seen in Cherry's hands that first time
they met at the Temple of Heaven.
It was hard to drive at a walking pace,
so he rolled a hundred yards behind,
close to the curb, trying not to lose the small, quick figure,
as bicycles swarmed behind him,
mesmerized by the Hello Kitty bobbleheads.
When Shirley arrived at the school gates,
a group of girls ran to meet her,
Weng used his binoculars to watch them
hug and jump in the playground with joy.

That afternoon, Weng stayed in the hotel and
watched a film about a girl, her grandfather, and a bird.
Then he went down to the spa on the mezzanine level,
but a different masseuse was working,
so he made an excuse and went back to his room.
Next morning, Weng wanted to follow Cherry again,
but he felt too awkward spying on a child he didn't even know.
So he stayed in his room watching more television,
and took his meals early.
In the evening, he walked around the lobby of the hotel,
then found somewhere to sit
and read through Cherry's old text messages.
The foreigners who had laughed and drank toasts were gone,
and the waiters were just standing around looking idle.

A fresh wave of guests arrived overnight,
and next morning the restaurant was packed
with international businesspeople
eating breakfast over newspapers and laptop computers.
Weng left the hotel early and drove around Ningbo,
stopping to eat fish-head soup in a small park.
He decided that, since he had followed Shirley to school once,
he could follow her home once, and so arrived a full hour
before dismissal to secure a good parking spot.
As he waited, Weng smelled something
and realized the plastic container of fish-head soup
left over from lunch had split and leaked
into the Rolls-Royce's Blenheim carpet.
He collected as many bones as he could,
and put them in the wood-grain tray.

With half an hour to go before the school bell,
Weng sat watching passersby
through the car's parking cameras.
Although he was afraid of how it would make him feel,
he more than ever wanted to catch a glimpse
of Cherry's husband
so that his hopes might be crushed entirely
and he could return to Beijing.
Perhaps Shirley's father traveled for work?
Or was he bedridden?
Or crippled and able to move only one eyelid?

When Shirley appeared at the school gates
(with no father to meet her),
Weng felt self-conscious and awkward again,
but started the engine,
and resolved that once she was home safe
and through the outside door of her apartment building,
he would go straight back to the hotel and pack for Beijing.
However, at some point Shirley turned off the usual path
and Weng lost sight of her.
He stopped and got out of the car.
Perhaps she had gone down one of the side streets
with the idea of taking a shortcut?
Then, suddenly, there she was in the doorway of a shop,
holding a bag of Ningbo fried batter.

"Here," she said, holding out the bag to Weng.

"You can only get this in Ningbo."

Weng didn't move.

"Go on," Shirley said. "Don't be shy."

Weng took the bag.

"Why did you follow me to school the other day?"

"You're mistaken," Weng told her. "I don't—"

"No mistake," Shirley said, holding up her phone,

"I recorded you."

"Your phone takes video?"

"We don't have to play games," Shirley said. "I know who you are.
My mother told me about you, but never said that you were rich!"

"I'm not rich."

"Modest too!"

Then Shirley pulled him toward the car.

"Wait till my grandparents see you. They will be so surprised!"

"No," Weng said. "Stop! What are you doing, I'm a stranger—
you shouldn't be talking to me, get away!"

But Shirley was already climbing
into the backseat of the Rolls-Royce.

"What's that smell?" she said.

Weng tapped on the glass. "You have to get out."

Shirley wrinkled her nose. "Smells like a hutong in here!"

Then people were starting to look
so Weng got in and drove away quickly.

"It's like you're kidnapping me!" Shirley said.

"I'm stopping at the next corner and you have to get out!"

But Shirley said if he did that, she would scream.

"Just take me home," she told him. "You know the way."

When they were near her apartment Shirley asked if Weng
would drive her to school the next morning.

"Absolutely not," he said. "No way. Impossible."

"Aren't you here to surprise Mom for her birthday?"

Weng looked at Shirley in his mirror. "But her birthday was
eight months ago, and she lives in Beijing."

Shirley gave a sly smile and leaned back in her seat.

"So you are my missing father."

"Your father is missing?" Weng said with more hopefulness
than he intended.

"Not anymore," Shirley said, "Unless you're trying
to keep your return secret?"

"Yes! Yes! I am trying to keep everything secret."

"But you'll still drive me to school tomorrow?"

"No way."

"If you don't, I'll tell my grandparents that you're back."

"But I have to be somewhere. I have important business."

"But you're rich, Dad! Take the day off—take the year off!"

"How will you explain to your friends and grandparents the strange man driving you to school?"

"I'll say that I won a competition."

"Funny," Weng said. "That's what I usually say too."

"I'll tell anyone who asks I won Bunny Pops Bingo."

"What's Bunny Pops?"

"As my father, you may as well learn that Bunny Pops Bingo is my favorite app, which is also a candy now. I'll explain to everyone that I won a Bunny Pops Bingo prize jackpot of a Rolls-Royce to drive me to and pick me up from school for as long as you want to keep everything secret."

"I don't know," Weng said. "Seems too complicated—and how is it connected to Bunny Pops, exactly?"

"I've been playing Bingo since I was three on my phone and there are prizes—it's simple. I'll get you the app if you want—do you have a phone?"

"Yes," Weng said. "A very good one, actually."

After getting out of the car, Shirley tapped on the glass.
Weng pushed a button and the window
whispered into the door.
For a few moments, Shirley just stood there looking at him.
"All this time you were gone," she said finally, "I thought it was
my fault because you had wanted a boy and got me instead."

When Weng got back to the hotel, he had to lie down.
Then, about eleven P.M., he got another foot massage
because the masseuse he knew was back.
"What's it like being a parent?" he asked her.
"It's hard," the woman said.
"Because you don't have time for yourself anymore?"
"No," the masseuse laughed. "Because you worry so much."
"About money?"
"About them getting hurt. Money is just a side worry."
After the massage Weng asked someone at the front desk
to bring his car around.
By dawn, he had driven to over a dozen all-night supermarkets,
buying every box of Bunny Pops he could find and emptying
the contents into the backseat.
The next morning, Shirley couldn't believe it,
"I feel like I really have won!"

When Weng went to pick her after school,
Shirley had someone with her.
"This is Melody, my best friend."
Weng glared at Shirley.
"What?" She shrugged. "I'm just so excited you're back."
Then Melody got into the Rolls-Royce and said:
"It's so nice of your dad to take us
to Chenghuang Miao market for new shoes."
"I thought I was driving you home!"
"Too late—I already texted Grandma to say I was going to
Melody's house, and she texted to say
she was coming to my house."
Melody clapped her hands. "So we're free to shop
all night or until the money runs out."
"Which will be never," Shirley laughed, unwrapping a Bunny
Pop and handing it to her friend. "Right, Dad?"

An hour later, Weng found himself negotiating
the price of girls' sneakers with a very short woman who
wouldn't budge on the price.
"You shouldn't argue prices," Melody said loudly,
"when you drive a Rolls-Royce."
They walked around the night market
then had dinner in the back of the car
so that Weng could demonstrate the karaoke system.
The girls sang songs like "Planting Trees" and "Tadpoles Lost."
Weng chose "Blue Flowers."

That night, before going to sleep, Shirley made a drawing.
Here we are . . ., she said to herself as the crayon
moved across paper . . .
. . . *Shirley and Melody at Chenghuang Miao market*
with Dad buying new shoes. . . .
They were barefoot in the picture
and their feet were blue with cold.
Then she drew the shop, and the stout shopkeeper
with a gray coat and the mole on her cheek.
Everyone had hearts for eyes.
Their new shoes in the drawing were made of gold.
. . . *Now we're in Dad's car, eating noodles and singing. . . .*
Then Shirley picked her best red crayon and wrote to her
mother, using all the correct strokes to say,
It's time to be a family again.

十二

A few days later,
Shirley offered to show Weng a park where people sing.
One group was about to start an opera
and its members were setting out colorful stools
for anyone willing to stay.
Weng bought Shirley an ice cream.
"Wish Melody was here," she said.
"It's good to have a best friend."
Shirley nodded. "Do you have one?"
Weng thought about it. "I used to."
"What happened to them?"
"We no longer speak."
"That's weird."
"When you care about someone, Shirley, you do what is right
for them—which may not be what you want
or what makes you happy."
Shirley licked her ice cream. "Is that why you
had to go away for so long?"
"And why I have to go away again," Weng said.

On the walk back to the car,
they stood for a moment by the lake.
"I wonder if people long ago thought a part of them was trapped
in the water?" Weng said.
"Look," Shirley said. "We're trapped together."
He knew that leaving was the right thing to do
but could not bring himself to say he was not her father;
it was a lie that felt true.

When they pulled up outside her apartment home,
Shirley was crying and wouldn't take off her seat belt.
"You must go back now to your grandparents."
"I know what you're doing," Shirley said.
"You're going to Beijing."
"Shirley, please go now."
"Why can't I come?"
"I can't tell you without lying."
"When will you be back?"
"I don't know," Weng said. "Take these Bunny Pops
to remember me."
"I don't want them," Shirley said. "I want to come to Beijing
with you and surprise Mom."

When he got back to the hotel,
Weng asked the porter to find him a dictionary.
"I don't think we have one. We used to, but it's gone now."
"Never mind then," Weng said turning,
but the porter held his arm gently.
"Why don't you tell me the word, Mr. Fun, and I'll look it up on
the Internet, print it out, then hand it to you silently so no one
has to know?"
Once back in his room, Weng read the character over and over:

爸爸 ba ba (he who uses an ax to cut wood to warm the home)

It didn't say anything about blood,
and so Weng wondered if there was a chance
it could mean anyone.

Then he packed his bag,
Left an envelope with three Bunny Pops and ten thousand yuan
for the foot masseuse, and began the long journey back to Beijing.

In a gas station café someone had left a straw hat.

Weng picked it up, imagined the owner touching his head,

the sensation of unexpected loss.

Then about halfway home, he almost crashed into another car

because there was someone sitting in the backseat.

"Stay calm," the figure said. "Focus on driving."

But Weng was in shock. "What are you doing in my car!" he

screamed. "Did you get in at the service station?"

"No, no, nothing like that," the shadow told him. "by the way, is

this the new Phantom?"

Blinking several times to ensure he wasn't dreaming,

Weng said nervously that it was.

"It seems different somehow," the voice said,

"I can't put my finger on it. . . ."

"It's the floor model with karaoke upgrade."

"Ah that must be it! My son's has the humidor,

and the picnic set—but not the karaoke."

"What do you mean?" Weng said. "Your son has a Rolls-Royce?

Did you get into the wrong one?"

"Not exactly, Fun Weng. I am the ghost pig farmer of

Guanshan—and late father of Mr. Yi."

Weng turned in disbelief, and the car veered toward a low stone

wall.

"Better watch what you're doing," Mr. Yi's late father laughed.
"Or we'll both be sitting back here with all these Bunny Pops
and the fishy smell."

"Have I done something wrong?"

"No, no," the ghost said. "I'm here because
you've done something right."

"Do you appear to your son like this?"

"Of course not! It would be much too complicated,
seeing as I'm technically dead."

"But you're here now," Weng pointed out,
"in the back of my Rolls-Royce."

"No," said the late Mr. Yi, "I've just willed myself into the shape
I had before so that I can ask you to help my son."

"I don't understand. I can see you. . . ."

"Okay, watch this," said the ghost and disappeared.

A moment later the Hello Kitty bobbleheads on the back
window opened their mouths and began
singing the Chinese national anthem.

Then the ghost reappeared in the shape of Mr. Yi.

"I'm just a spirit—conjured in part by you. But listen to me now, Fun Weng," the ghost said. "I'm worried about my son. He is deeply unhappy, and very alone. At this rate, he'll never meet anyone, and the living Mrs. Yi and I want grandchildren."

"But you're dead."

"That doesn't matter—a grandparent's wish for grandchildren goes beyond the grave."

"But what can I do? How can I help?"

"Be a friend to him, Weng, that's all. Reach out to him when you get back and his life will begin changing for the better."

"I'll do my best."

"Good," the spirit said. "Just be a friend and the rest will take care of itself—these things I know—

but make haste, please. . . ."

"I will call the moment I get back."

"Thank you," the voice said. "You are *my* Golden Helper."

About the time Weng returned to Beijing,
Cherry got the drawing from her daughter in the mail,
and texted her Uncle Ping immediately:

丈夫回来了!
非常富有吗?
真倒霉☹

HUSBAND RETURNED!
VERY RICH?
WHAT BAD LUCK ☹

Uncle Ping texted back:

给雪莉打电话。问问她事情进展地怎么样了。
离婚还有可能吗? ☺生活就像跳舞

CALL SHIRLEY. FIND OUT WHAT'S GOING ON.
DIVORCE STILL POSSIBLE? ☺ LIFE ABOUT DANCING

When Cherry telephoned her daughter,
the terrible news was confirmed.
"Yes, Mom, it's true!" Shirley exclaimed. "And Dad's on his way
right now from Ningbo to get you!"
After the call, Shirley put on her silk scarf,
then sat a long time on her bed touching the knot,
staring out through hanging clothes
at the night sky.

The next day, when a Rolls-Royce Phantom crawled
through Cherry's hutong district, past the bicycles,
and the women sleeping, and the steam from pots,
people wondered what was happening.
Was someone buying up property to build another mall?
Had a neighbor won a competition?
Gotten lucky in Macao?
Or inherited a vast sum from an unmarried great-aunt
in Hong Kong?

At first Cherry wouldn't answer the door,
but the person kept knocking
then a voice came through the wood.
"I was wondering if you would like to ballroom with me? I
think you would be successful if you tried."
Cherry touched the back of the door with both hands.
"We're not getting any younger," the voice said.
"We might as well try."
After some time, the handle turned,
and the door opened slowly.
There was Weng with his arms in position.
"Don't look at your feet," he said as they began to move.
"Look at me."
After a few times around the car,
old people appeared from nowhere and joined in.

Later on, over dinner, Cherry laughed at the story of Shirley and Melody buying new shoes at the night market. Although she was ashamed of it, Cherry admitted to Weng how glad she was that her real husband was still missing. "Though a divorce could take years," she warned him.

Weng thought the most important thing was for mother and
daughter to reunite. "Take some time off," he said.
"I'll drive you to Ningbo and you can explain
how I am just a friend and there was a mix-up. Then Shirley can
come to Beijing and live with you."
"But her school . . ."
"There are schools here too," Weng said. "And night markets."
"What about her grandparents?"
"Bring them as well . . . we can all be unemployed together."

When they arrived at the factory where Cherry worked,
her supervisor and coworkers wanted to know
if this was the man who had bought Cherry
such a pretty silk scarf?
Once Weng had explained his good fortune,
the boss agreed to give Cherry time off,
but wanted a favor in return.
"My son is partially sighted and attends a school for the blind.
He loves cars but has never had a chance to experience a
nice one. Would you take him for a ride in your Rolls-Royce
sometime?"

That night Weng tried calling Mr. Yi again.

He had been telephoning daily since his return from Ningbo but with no answer.

This time his secretary picked up and said he was on a business trip—would not be back for many days.

"A business trip?"

"Yes, Mr. Yi is in New England."

"Where's that?"

"I don't know, maybe next to the old one?"

"Well, please tell him it is extremely urgent that we speak."

That night, as Weng and Cherry packed the car for Ningbo,
Shirley was planning a trip of her own.
She had taken a picture of a train schedule with her phone,
and found times for the early morning express to Beijing.
Sneaking on shouldn't be too hard, she thought.
Children always find a way.
She wanted to surprise her mother and win her father's
admiration for embarking on such a daring journey.
Shirley kissed her grandparents many times that night,
knowing they would suffer when her breakfast went cold.
She also kissed the photograph of her mother and drew hearts
on the plastic glass for eyes.

Seven hundred miles north of Ningbo, on a lonely stretch of the
Rongwu Expressway, Cherry noticed someone sitting
in the backseat and started screaming.
Weng glanced quickly, expecting to see Mr. Yi's father,
but instead it was the face of a man he didn't know,
wearing a sad, vacant expression.
Cherry was so hysterical, Weng had to pull
to the side of the road.
When the car stopped, she flung open the door
and ran into the middle of a field.

It was hard to speak, but at last she was able
to tell Weng who the man in the backseat was.
When Cherry was ready to listen, Weng told her about Mr. Yi's
father, and how he'd turned the Hello Kitty bobbleheads into a
choir.
Cherry just couldn't understand how it was possible.
Weng didn't know either.
"Maybe it came with the karaoke package?"

"We should find out what he has to say," Weng said. "Get back in the car before he disappears."

When they were on the highway again, Cherry undid her seat belt, and turned around to face the husband

she had not seen for so many years.

"Are you alive?" she said.

The ghost closed his eyes and shook his head from side to side.

Weng asked how it happened.

"Knocked off my bicycle by a vegetable truck."

"Even though I thought I didn't love you anymore," Cherry told the ghost, "seeing you like this has brought some of the old tenderness back."

"None of what happened was your fault," the ghost confessed. "I lived drunk and I died drunk. But listen, now. I have come back to tell you something important. Right now, Shirley is making her way through the dark streets to Ningbo station, where she plans to board an early train. You have to get there before the 5:13 A.M. leaves for Beijing."

"But that's only five hours!" Cherry exclaimed,

"and we're not even halfway—"

"I know," the ghost said, drifting toward Fun Weng,

"Which is another reason I'm here—now you know why they call it the Phantom."

Within a few seconds, the Phantom had reached its top speed.
Any cars they passed shook violently in a flash of lights,
leaving the occupants to wonder whether they had been
brushed by a low-flying jet,
or were part of a military experiment.
When they arrived at the outskirts of Ningbo,
it was twenty minutes before Shirley's train was due to depart.
"I'm going now," the ghost told them. "I hope I've been more
use in death than I was in life." Cherry reached out her hand,
but the ghost didn't move.
"My body was never identified, but there's a police record of the
accident, so you should be able to get married."
"Thanks for helping us," Cherry said.
"Hurry now," the voice instructed.
"There's less time than you think."

They dumped the Rolls in a vacant bus lane and ran into the
station. Weng took one platform while Cherry took another.
When it came time for the train to leave, there was still no sign
of Shirley, so Weng told the guard,
who used his radio to delay the train.
But after an hour's search, no child was found.
The train staff promised to keep an eye out, and to alert police
when they arrived in Beijing. Cherry wondered if perhaps her
daughter had changed her mind, and was back home in bed—
or even if her late husband's ghost was up to no good.

When they returned to the car,
a gang of police was waiting for them.
"Why did you leave your car running in a bus lane with a child
by herself?" one of them said accusingly, stepping aside to
reveal Shirley in the backseat breakfasting on a Bunny Pop.
Another policeman shook his head in reproach. "You are rich
and must learn what it means to be good parents."
Then Cherry got into the backseat
and kissed her daughter all over.
"Please tell me you're not a ghost," she said.
"How did you find the car?" Weng asked as they drove away.
Shirley said a kind old farmer had asked for help
to find his train to Guanshan,
but instead had guided her through the crowds until
she was next to the big car she knew so well.
"Did he say anything else?" Weng said.
"Yes," Shirley said. "He asked me if I like pigs then
said his son is not in New England after all.
I just smiled. Old people get so confused."

十三

When the three of them got back to Beijing the next day,
Weng drove over to Mr. Yi's office.
The secretary did not give much information,
and did not recognize Weng, so he told her
that he knew Mr. Yi was in Beijing,
and had orders to deliver his car.
The secretary looked out the window
at the black Rolls-Royce below.
"Okay," she said. "Here's the address where he is."
It took a long time through Beijing traffic
to reach Mr. Yi's apartment.
Weng buzzed several times before a sad, small voice
filled the security system.
The elevator went straight up and opened on his apartment.

Mr. Yi was in a bathrobe drinking Scotch. He seemed angry.

"What are you doing here?"

"I was worried about you, Mr. Yi."

"About me? Well, it's not the best time. . . ."

"May I come in?" Weng said.

"No."

"Please?"

"What do you want to come in for?"

"To talk about Golden Helper."

"Is everything okay?"

"Yes, I just want to come in."

"Bad timing."

"Well, at least let me come in and make you some tea."

"Maybe tomorrow, Fun Weng,
we can meet at the hotel on Goldfish Lane."

"I'd like to come in now, if that's okay."

"I'm busy!" Mr. Yi snapped. "Why now?"

Weng glanced down at Mr. Yi's velvet slippers. "Because the ghost of your father appeared in the backseat of my car and begged that I come over and save you from a childless life of loneliness and depression."

Mr. Yi just stared at him.

"Do you believe in ghosts, Mr. Yi?"

After dinner, Weng tried to suggest some changes for Mr. Yi,
maybe a move to somewhere more peaceful near his mother, or
ballroom lessons in the park,
or some new business venture. . . .
"That's the last thing I need," Mr. Yi said. "More business!"
"But I thought you loved it," Weng said, "And you're so good at
making money."
"You are mistaken," Mr. Yi said. "I love putting things together.
Making things work. Seeing things come into the world from
nothing—money is just a result of this."
"Like with Golden Helper II?"
"Exactly," Mr. Yi said. "Good old blind Mr. Fun."
"What else can you do, then?" Weng asked, thinking aloud.
"What excited you most as a boy?"
Mr. Yi considered the question carefully.
"When my father used to give me old radios or tractor parts to
take apart, back on the pig farm. I used to love getting my hands
oily and discovering how things worked. But I'm
older now, Fun Weng, and such a long way
from the happiness of childhood."

After putting Mr. Yi to bed, Weng texted Cherry to say that
everything was all right then tidied the apartment,
bagging empty bottles,
and putting leftover food in the trash.
Before going home, he scribbled out a note
and left it on the table.

亲爱的易先生:

明天我会给您的秘书打电话，告诉您我们见面的时间和地
点。请穿旧衣服，就像农村养猪的农民穿的那种军装。

你的朋友
翁

Dear Mr. Yi,
Tomorrow I'm going to call your secretary with a date and an
address of somewhere I want you to meet me. Dress in something old, like the army clothes pig farmers wear in the coun-
tryside.

Your friend
Weng

The next morning, Weng called Cherry's old boss at the factory, then got in touch with the Beijing School for Blind Children that his son attended.

The principal of the school listened to Fun Weng's proposal, then suggested they meet in person at her office.

After a tour of the facilities, Weng reiterated his willingness to make a donation, but humbly requested that a gifted engineer he knew

be allowed to visit the school and give

elementary lessons in mechanics.

"Of course!" Said the principal, "We always welcome skilled volunteers, as we do donations of any sort.

Did you have a figure in mind, Mr. Fun?"

"Yes," Weng said, "but there isn't enough space on the check for all the zeros, so I'll be sending cash if that's okay."

The principal was silent for a moment, then burst out laughing.

"For a moment there, Mr. Fun, I thought you were serious."

The next morning, three hundred Golden Helper mechanisms,
three hundred basic tool sets, thirty thousand Bunny Pops,
and a convoy of armored cars were dispatched
to the Beijing School for Blind Children.

A year later, Weng and Mr. Yi bought an additional
eight Rolls-Royce Phantoms to use as school buses,
and Uncle Ping joined the faculty as professor of karaoke.
It was also agreed that continuing profits from Golden Helper II
would be funneled directly into the building
and staffing of schools for disabled children across the globe,
which is exactly the sort of thing blind Mr. Fun had in mind
as he folded pieces of newspaper in a special way
at the kitchen table one night,
his wife and son asleep in the next room,
rolling around in dreams
on the old spring bed.

Author's Note

A version of "The Menace of Mile End" appeared on Book-track (Soundtracks for Books) in 2013.

A version of "The Muse" was commissioned by the Waldorf Astoria in 2013, and appears on its website and was printed in *Waldorf Astoria Magazine*.

A version of "Private Life of a Famous Chinese Film Director" appeared in Issue 27 of *AnOther Magazine*.

Acknowledgments

The author wishes to acknowledge the following people:

Amy Baker; Betty; Joshua Bodwell; Bryan Le Boeuf; my dear brother, Darren Booy, and his wife, Raha; Joan and Stephen Booy; Catrin Brace and the Welsh Assembly Government; Ken Browar; Laura Brown; David Bruson; Jonathan Burnham; Cherry; Li Chow; Denise and James Connelly; Rejean Daigneault; Trent Duffy; Cynthia and Justin Ellis; Wolfgang Egger; Dr. Shilpi Epstein; Laurie Fink; Foxy; Dani Gill; Dr. Bruce Gelb; Primal Groudon; Jen Hart; Dolores Henry; Gregory Henry; Nancy Horner; Mr. Howard; Prof. Huang; Jig; Zach Johnson; Jermyn St. Journal; Carlos Juarbe; David Kaplan; Jamie Kerner; Hilary Knight; Sam Levinson; Dorit Matthews; Megatronus; Mr. & Mrs. Samuel Morris III; Michael Morrison; Lukas Ortiz; Deborah Ory; Wendy and Jon Paton; Peninsula Hotel, Beijing; Peng Lun; Qu Zhongru; Jonathan D. Rabinowitz; Ashwin Rattan; Tamara Rawitt; Rob; Rolls-Royce Motor Cars, China; Marcell Rosenblatt; Lori and Ted Schultz; Lisa Sharkey; Ivan Shaw and Lisa Von Weise Shaw; Dmitri Shostakovich; Oriana Siska, Tuesday; Violet; Virginia Stanley; Jeremy Strong; the Vilcek Foundation; Waldorf Astoria Hotels; Mojo Wang; Sherry Wasserman; Sylvia Beach Whitman at Shakespeare & Company; and Georgi Zhikharev.

These amazing individuals at Conville & Walsh:

Jake Smith-Bosanquet; Alexander Cochran; Alexandra McNicoll.

Extra special thanks for the emotional support, close friendship, and editorial feedback of Lucas Hunt, Carrie Kania, and Cal Morgan; and of course my wonderful wife, Christina Daigneault, and our brilliant daughter, Madeleine.